THE
ARCTIC
CODE

— BOOK ONE —
in the
DARK GRAVITY SEQUENCE

THE
ARCTIC
CODE

Matthew J. Kirby

BALZER + BRAY
An Imprint of HarperCollinsPublishers

Balzer + Bray is an imprint of HarperCollins Publishers.

The Arctic Code
Copyright © 2015 by HarperCollins Publishers
For information address HarperCollins Children's Books,
a division of HarperCollins Publishers,
195 Broadway, New York, NY 10007.
www.harpercollinschildrens.com

Library of Congress Cataloging-in-Publication Data
Kirby, Matthew J., date, author.
   The Arctic code / Matthew J. Kirby. — First edition.
       pages   cm. — (Dark gravity sequence ; book one)
   Summary: The Earth is in the grip of a new Ice Age, and when twelve-
year-old Eleanor's scientist mother disappears in the Arctic, Eleanor sets off
on a dangerous journey to find her—and uncovers a mystery, a crime, and
evidence that Earth has been visited by extraterrestrials.
   ISBN 978-0-06-222487-3 (hardcover : alk. paper)
   1. Glacial epoch—Juvenile fiction. 2. Scientists—Juvenile fiction.
3. Mothers and daughters—Juvenile fiction. 4. Adventure stories.
5. Extraterrestrial beings—Juvenile fiction. [1. Science fiction. 2. Glacial
epoch—Fiction. 3. Scientists—Fiction. 4. Mothers and daughters—
Fiction. 5. Adventure and adventurers—Fiction. 6. Extraterrestrial
beings—Fiction.]   I. Title.
PZ7.K633528Ar 2015   2014030622
[813.6]—dc23   CIP
                                                                AC

Typography by Carla Weise
15 16 17 18 19   CG/RRDH   10 9 8 7 6 5 4 3 2 1
❖
First Edition

For Jaime, who brought such light and
warmth into my world

CHAPTER 1

ELEANOR STEPPED UP TO THE EDGE, FRAMED BY THE OPEN-ing in the cinder-block wall, and looked down over the construction site. An icy, brutal wind whipped and slashed the plastic sheeting at her feet, which stretched downward from her at an angle, two stories to the ground, forming a transparent slope.

"I really don't think you should do this, Ellie."

Eleanor looked over her shoulder, back to where Claire and Jenna huddled together, teeth chattering amid the building's bare bones. Her friends had left their outer coats at home, and their inner coats weren't strong enough to stop the cold up here. But Eleanor had warned them about the temperature.

1

"This is probably the last sub day we'll have this spring," she said. Subzero days were common enough in other parts of the southern United States, but they might only get a dozen each year in Phoenix. *"And,"* Eleanor continued, "Mr. Goering announced they're going to finish this construction next week." The plastic tent was only there temporarily to protect the fresh masonry. *"Plus,* it's a Sunday and there's no one working here. This is the only shot we have."

"The only shot *you* have." Claire shook her head, the little pom-poms on her knitted cap batting at each other. "I was never doing this."

Eleanor cocked her head to the side with a crooked smile. "Right. You'll just stand there and watch me do it."

"That's right." Jenna nodded in mock condescension.

Eleanor shook her head. "Whatever, you guys. Just bring me that fan, okay?"

The two girls groaned, clapped their gloved hands to warm their fingers, and reached for the industrial fan Eleanor had "borrowed" from the school's custodian. While they dragged it up to the ledge, Eleanor crossed the cement floor, threading the building's metal and wooden framing, to the fire hose. No one had bothered to lock the glass case yet, since this new

2

wing the city was adding onto their school wouldn't have students for several weeks.

But the hose had water, and the fan had power. That was all she needed.

Eleanor wrenched the hose's nozzle out of its cradle and walked backward away from the wall, tugging the coiled hose free. It was heavier than she'd expected it to be, and she heaved and panted as she dragged the nozzle to the ledge, where the frigid wind nipped at the insides of her lungs.

"Seriously, Ellie." Claire's glance flicked to the steep drop-off. "It's too high, this is crazy."

"Just watch." Eleanor pointed. "Jenna, go over there, and when I say, you turn on the water."

Jenna rolled her eyes. "Ellie—"

"Just do it, okay?"

Jenna sighed and stomped over to the fire-hose valve.

Eleanor smiled and flicked on the fan. Construction dust and debris stirred on the floor around them as the blast and roar picked up. Eleanor put her hand in front of the fan, spreading her fingers wide, testing its force. The air pushed hard, making it difficultto keep her hand there. This was going to work.

She picked up the nozzle and shoved it tight against the back of the fan, right where it sucked the air in.

Then she looked at Jenna.

"Now!" Eleanor shouted over the storm sound of the fan.

Jenna cranked the valve, and Eleanor watched a traveling bulge as the hose expanded like a digesting snake. She braced herself as a moment later the water reached the nozzle and hissed into the spinning blades.

On the other side, the fan shot a ragged mist into the air, and with the temperature waiting below zero, the water droplets froze into little crystals, instantly.

Snow.

It fell onto the plastic sheet below, some of it sticking, some sliding downward, until a trail of white ran from their high perch almost to the ground below. Eleanor kept her makeshift snow machine churning until the fan sputtered, coughed, and gagged to a stop, its blades and insides encrusted with ice.

"That's enough!" Eleanor called to Jenna.

Her friend turned the fire-hose valve, and the water from the nozzle dribbled off.

Eleanor dragged the hose out of the way, and then she moved the fan. Jenna walked over to stand by Claire, and the two of them had gone from looking worried and annoyed to looking scared.

"Okay, it worked," Claire said. "You're a genius. Can we go now?"

"Not until I ride down my hill." Eleanor marched over to where she'd leaned a sled against the wall. She didn't want to let her friends see, but her hands were shaking. Her rapid heartbeat had begun to steal the edges of her breath.

"Ellie," Jenna said, "you can't do this. You're gonna kill yourself."

"No, I'm not." Eleanor propped the sled in front of her, right at the ledge. "There's snow down there for a bit of cushion. That'll help. And then the angle of the plastic at the bottom will just shoot me out across the ground." She used her flattened hand to demonstrate the motion. "I'll come to a gradual stop."

"You mean a *sudden* stop!" Jenna said.

"Guys, it's sledding. People do this all the time. Just . . . not in Phoenix."

The wind had turned more aggressive, somehow. Like it was taunting Eleanor. Daring her to follow through with her plan. But now that she stood here at the edge, ready to do it, she could also hear her mother asking just what exactly she was thinking. Her mom would go ballistic over the sled part, of course. But she would probably smile wryly over the snow machine.

"Don't do it," Claire said.

"I have to." Eleanor backed up and let the sled fall flat to the ground.

5

"You're a freak!" Jenna said.

It wasn't the first time Eleanor had heard that. She had plenty of friends, but she had a reputation for being . . . different. Even though she'd long since accepted that she *was* different, it still hurt to have someone call her a freak to her face.

No doubt this stunt would be all over the school before they were even back from break, but that wasn't why Eleanor was up there, sitting down on a sled, scooting right up to the ledge. She didn't care what people would say about this afterward. It was about what Eleanor said to herself, right now. How she felt about herself in this moment. It was about the drive inside her, almost an itch. There was only one way to scratch it, and this was the part of Eleanor no one understood. Not even her mom.

The sled scraped across the cement floor as Eleanor jostled into position, its nose now jutting out into space.

Jenna clutched her stomach. "Oh my God, I'm gonna hurl."

"Go do it over there," Eleanor said. She reached forward with both hands and grabbed the ledge of the building to either side. All she had to do was heave herself forward, and she'd launch over the edge and down the plastic slope. She took a deep breath.

"Please, Ellie." Claire's voice broke. "Don't—"

"STOP!" a male voice shouted. "WHAT ARE YOU DOING?"

Eleanor whipped a look back. Mr. Goering, the principal, rushed toward them through the building with a couple of cops trailing behind him. Eleanor only had a moment before they reached her and she lost her chance.

"Don't even think about it, Miss Perry!" Mr. Goering shouted, red-faced. "If you're still alive at the bottom, I'll expel you!"

That caused Eleanor to hesitate. Kids in Phoenix sat on long waiting lists to get into public schools. With the refugees pouring into the city every week, there just wasn't enough room for all of them. If Eleanor got expelled, she wouldn't get back in, and there was no way they could afford private school. Her mom would be devastated.

That moment of hesitation was all Mr. Goering needed. In the next instant, Eleanor felt his big hands on her shoulders, pulling her away from the ledge.

"It was all Ellie's idea," Jenna said, her voice a high-pitched squeal.

Eleanor rolled her eyes as she got to her feet. Jenna was always the first to crack.

"Of that I have no doubt," Mr. Goering said. He

was wearing only his inner coat, too, his customary comb-over a fluttering wisp on the wrong side. He must have rushed to the school in a hurry.

The two cops had stepped away, one of them speaking into a staticky radio clipped at his shoulder.

Eleanor turned to Mr. Goering. "How did you find out I was here?"

"You thought no one in the neighborhood would notice?" Mr. Goering pulled her farther into the building, as if the ledge made him nervous. "I received three phone calls asking why there seemed to be a snowstorm blowing from inside my school."

Eleanor hadn't figured it would be that obvious.

"Honestly, Miss Perry." Mr. Goering shook his head. "These antics of yours must stop, or one of these days the consequences will be dire. What would your mother say if I called her?"

Eleanor couldn't keep the scoff from her voice. "Good luck with that, Mr. Goering. She's still in the Arctic, and honestly, I think she has more important things on her mind."

"And that is the only reason you have enjoyed my forbearance," he said. "But mark my words, after today you are but one tiny infraction away from expulsion. I don't care how small. If I hear that you have so much as littered, you're done at my school. Do you hear me?"

8

The mention of expulsion hit Eleanor just as hard the second time. She dropped her gaze to the ground, deflated. "Yes, sir."

"Good." Mr. Goering breathed in deeply. "And now, these two fine gentlemen will take the three of you into custody."

"What?" Claire said. "Why?"

"Trespassing." One of the cops stepped forward. "Destruction of property."

"But it was all *her!*" Jenna's glare brought up a twinge of guilt in Eleanor, but she was able to ignore it. The three of them had been friends long enough for Claire and Jenna to know *exactly* what it meant to hang out with Eleanor. They got a bystander rush out of it, too. This would blow over like it always did.

"We'll sort it out at the station," the cop said. "With your parents."

That thought caused a different kind of guilt that lingered. With her mom in the Arctic, the police would have to call Uncle Jack, and he didn't need this. Eleanor cast a final glance at the ledge, the iced-over fan, and the sled, and let the cop lead her away.

⟢ CHAPTER ⟣
2

UNCLE JACK SAID VERY LITTLE AT THE POLICE STATION. Mostly, he just nodded along with whatever the cop was saying, very slowly, as if the earth's gravity had doubled. He was wearing his blue coveralls, which meant he'd been at work when they called him. Uncle Jack was always picking up extra shifts when he could, even on the weekends.

"Young lady," the cop said, "do you know how lucky you are Mr. Goering decided not to press charges?"

He expected an answer. Eleanor sat up straight. "I do, sir."

"This could have been a lot worse for you," the cop said.

"I know," Eleanor said.

The cop directed the next thing he said to Uncle Jack, and Eleanor mostly ignored what he was saying. They weren't going to charge her, that was what mattered. Instead, she focused on the cop's cluttered desk, the half-buried photo of his family—wife, two kids, one of whom was squeezing an unhappy cat fighting to escape the frame. She focused on the water cooler burping every few minutes in the corner—

"Ellie," Uncle Jack said.

"Yeah?"

"Officer Nez asked you a question."

Eleanor looked in the cop's eyes. "Yes, sir?"

The cop angled his head, like he was stretching a kink in his neck. "I *said*, you're not going to set foot on your school's construction site, or any other site, ever again. Are you."

Uncle Jack was wrong, it wasn't a question. "No, sir."

"Good. I suppose you're free to leave."

"Thank you, Officer." Uncle Jack labored up from his chair, still fighting gravity. "What do you say, Ellie?"

"Thank you, Officer," Eleanor said.

"Have a nice day," the cop said, and Eleanor was pretty sure he wouldn't have said it any differently if she were being escorted out of here in handcuffs.

Eleanor followed Uncle Jack out of the office. She

walked behind him as he lumbered down the crowded hallway, clearing a path to the elevator, where he hit the ground floor button with his thick finger. They rode down listening to music that left Eleanor's brain itching, and then Uncle Jack led the way through the lobby, out to the heated parking garage, to their small, ancient electric car.

Eleanor wanted him to say something as they drove home, but he kept his eyes forward, right hand on the steering wheel, left hand rubbing his forehead. Eleanor looked out the window, at a billboard with a picture of a young mother reading a bedtime story to her two children by the soft glow of a lamp. The caption read, THIS MOMENT BROUGHT TO YOU BY THE GLOBAL ENERGY TRUST. The G.E.T. supplied power to, well, just about everyone.

They took the freeway, swinging around the maze of towering apartment buildings someone had long ago nicknamed the Ice Castles. They'd been built to house the thousands of refugees from Canada and the northern states who had been staggering into the city day after day, driven from their homes by the sheet of ice clawing its way south. Claire and Jenna lived in those apartments, and they hated it. Eleanor felt horrible when they talked about the crime, the plumbing and the power going out, the noise, the police raiding one of their neighbors down the hall in the middle of the night. But there were plenty of refugees who couldn't even get a place in Phoenix and had to keep moving south, hoping for a chance to cross the border into Mexico.

Past the Ice Castles, they entered into the suburbs where Eleanor lived. It wasn't the nicest neighborhood, but it was better than most people had it. Her mom was a geologist, and she'd been lucky enough to land a good job with Sohn International, a nonprofit oil company. And in today's world, oil meant the ultimate job security.

They rolled down the narrow streets, past the identical narrow houses planted but inches apart, until they reached their home. Uncle Jack pulled into the driveway, left the engine running, the heat blasting, and cleared his throat.

"What would your mom say if she were here?" he asked. He sounded tired.

"She'd blame the Donor."

Uncle Jack chuckled. Eleanor's mom had never made time for romance but had always wanted a child, so she'd finally gone to a clinic. Eleanor's dad had been, and always would be, anonymous. That was just fine with Eleanor. She never even thought about him, except for those times her mother jokingly suggested that *he* was to blame for whatever it was about Eleanor that was irking Mom at that moment.

"And then what would she say?" Uncle Jack's voice sounded a bit lighter.

Eleanor shrugged. "She'd say she was disappointed in me. She'd say she was angry. But more than anything, she'd say she was glad I didn't kill myself." Eleanor swiveled toward him in her seat. "Which *totally* would not have happened, by the way. I had it under control."

"I'm sure you did."

"And she'd probably say it was 'devilishly clever' that I made my own snow."

He nodded. "Sounds like her. And since you already know what she would say, I don't think you need to waste the little time you get to talk with her making her say it."

"You mean . . ."

Uncle Jack ran his hand back and forth across the top of the steering wheel. "I mean we'll wait until she gets back from the Arctic to fill her in."

Eleanor smiled, relieved. "Thanks, Uncle Jack."

"No problem. But if you end up dead or in jail, I'll have to spill the beans. Got it?"

Eleanor laughed. "Got it." But her laughter faded quickly. "She was supposed to be home by now."

"I know. She'd be here if she could."

"But she hasn't even told us why she's still up there."

"She will when she can."

Eleanor gave a very small nod.

"Okay, get on inside. I gotta head back and finish my shift."

"I'm sorry, Uncle Jack. I didn't mean to mess up your job."

"It's okay. Maybe if I weren't working so many hours, I'd be around to keep you out of trouble."

"Oh, you think you can keep me out of trouble, do you?"

Uncle Jack shrugged. "I can try."

Eleanor opened her door. "Love you, Uncle Jack."

"Love you, too, Ell Bell."

Before she shut the door, he craned toward her across the passenger seat and looked up. "Oh, and Ellie?"

"Yeah?"

"For the record, I'm glad you didn't kill yourself." He winked.

Eleanor winked back and went inside.

Later that evening, Eleanor woke up to the sound of Uncle Jack in the kitchen downstairs. She'd lain down for a Sunday-afternoon nap shortly after he'd gone back to work, and opened her eyes to a room striped with evening sunlight through her blinds. It was a golden light, but cold like exposed metal. Her mom and Uncle Jack could remember a different sun, a warmer sun that reached through the cold and could even make you sweat. The distant sun Eleanor knew wasn't something she ever looked to for heat. She climbed out of bed and shivered a little, shuffled into her slippers, and left her room.

Their house was small—her mom insisted it was "cozy"—just the two bedrooms upstairs with a bathroom they shared when her mom wasn't in the Arctic, and the kitchen and living room downstairs. Her mom didn't exactly have an eye for design or decoration. The bare walls were the same hospital white they'd been when they'd first moved in ten years ago, though Eleanor had hung a changing parade of posters in her bedroom. Right now, she liked old movie banners, a phase her mom described as "Unintentionally Ironic Vintage."

Down in the kitchen, Uncle Jack stood at the stove wearing one of her mother's flowered aprons over his blue coveralls. Eleanor shook her head at the strings straining to reach around him, tied in a small and desperate knot high on his back.

He turned as she walked in. "Hungry?"

16

"It smells delicious."

"I can't make any promises." Uncle Jack always said that but never needed to. "They're supposed to be rosemary biscuits." He pulled on an oven mitt that matched the apron, part of a set. "I had to use the toaster oven to save gas, and the blasted thing won't go high enough for them to rise properly." He bent over, peering through the little smoky glass window. A few moments later, he seemed to sense something and pulled the baking sheet from the oven laden with plump, golden mounds.

"They look wonderful," Eleanor said. "And I'm sure they'll taste even better."

He frowned. "Get yourself a plate."

She grabbed a dish from the cupboard, and he served her up a biscuit.

"Here," he said. "I made a béchamel sauce and added a bit of prosciutto I found." He took her plate, split the biscuit with a fork, and ladled steaming gravy over it from a pot on the stove. Then he handed the plate back. "My own version of biscuits and gravy."

Eleanor shook her head. "Uncle Jack, you're going to get in trouble."

He waved her off with the oven mitt. "Don't worry, Ell Bell. This is all stuff they'd thrown away." Uncle Jack worked for an electrical company that serviced a lot of the mansions and hotels in Phoenix. Sometimes, his company contracted with the G.E.T., but years ago, he'd wanted to be a chef. That was before the Freeze— the new ice age—had really settled in.

Eleanor took her first bite, and it tasted so good she had to close her eyes. The biscuit was light and fluffy, in spite of the toaster oven, with just the right hint of rosemary, and the sauce was creamy and smoky. None of the kids she knew got to eat like this. The only people who could were the ones wealthy enough to import fresh produce and goods from South America and Africa, where anything could still be grown.

"What do you think?" Uncle Jack hadn't moved since passing her the plate.

"Amazing. I can't believe they'd throw this stuff away." She took another bite.

"A person's wealth is measured by what they can afford to throw away." He tried to reach back and untie the apron, and Eleanor watched him struggle for several moments, his shoulders all scrunched up, eyes on the ceiling, his mouth hanging open.

She grinned. "Would you like me to help you there?"

"Would you mind?"

Eleanor shook her head, still smiling, and went around behind him. He'd pulled the knot so tight, she ended up needing a fork to tease it loose.

"We need to get you a bigger apron," she said. "If you're—"

The chime cut through every noise in the house. It was a sound to which Eleanor's ears were constantly tuned. *Her Sync.*

Uncle Jack had heard it, too. "Go," he said. "Hurry."

Eleanor rushed up to the desk in her room. Her only connection to her mom was her Sync, a device used by the oil and energy companies so they'd have an instant, reliable method of communication that didn't require satellites or cell towers. The Sync, an advanced prototype, worked by something called *entanglement*. Tiny electrons in Eleanor's device perfectly matched their quantum twins in her mom's. The Sync couldn't transmit voice or video over this connection, but it could send text and other data. Over a normal cellular or Wi-Fi connection, it looked and acted like any other smartphone.

The screen flashed as Eleanor picked up the device.

<Hello, Eleanor! It's been so long. How are you?>

Eleanor smiled. It had been a long time, almost a week.

She typed. <Good! How r u?>

<I'm doing well, but I would be better if you didn't type in the text language of your generation. ;-}>

<Was that supposed to be a wink?>

<Yes. Did I not do it right?>

<It's this, Mom. ;)>

<;)>

<How cold is it up there right now?>

<Hang on.> . . . <minus 63 degrees Celsius>

Eleanor actually knew that already. She kept a daily eye on Arctic temperatures. <Brrrrr>

<You're right about that, sweetie.>

That temperature was fairly normal for this time of year, but winter had only begun. Temperatures would soon drop well below that. <Do you know when you're coming home?>

. . .

<Mom?>

<I'm not sure. Not yet, sweetie.>

<Do you know when you'll be sure?>

<I'm sorry, there's still work to do.>

Even through the Sync, Eleanor could tell there was something off. <Is everything ok?>

. . . <Yes, sorry. I'm just a bit tired and distracted, I guess. Tell me what's going on with you. How is school?>

Eleanor decided to let it go, for now. <I made a snow machine.>

<What?! How?>

<high-power fan + water hose + subzero temp = SNOW!!!>

<How devilishly clever of you.>

Eleanor smiled.

<That earned you an A, I assume? ;)>

Eleanor hesitated before typing. <Not exactly.>

<?>

<It wasn't for an assignment.>

<???>

<I'll tell you about it when you get home.>

. . . <You can imagine the look on my face right now, can't you?>

<Yes, Mom. But everything is ok.>

. . .

<MOM, IT IS OK.>

<All right. If you say so. I just hope you're going easy on your poor uncle Jack.>

Poor Uncle Jack. <I'm trying. But it's ok. He gets me.>

<Good. That makes one of us. ;)>

Eleanor chuckled. <Your wink is looking good.>

<Why thank you. My brilliant daughter taught me.>

<:)>

<Hold on, sweetie. Be right back.>

. . .

Eleanor stared at the screen as the wind picked up

outside. It always got windy after dark.

. . .

<Mom?>

<Yes, I'm here. But I have to go, sweetie. I love you.>

Already? <wait> They'd barely started talking. <y do u have to go?>

<We're prepping to head out onto the ice sheet tomorrow.>

<That sounds dangerous.>

<I'll be fine.> . . . <No need for you to worry.>

The feeling returned. There was something her mother wasn't telling her. If her mom was sitting here in person, Eleanor could probably guess what it was, but through the Sync, she had no idea.

<Mom, tell me.>

<Tell you what, sweetie?>

<What's going on?>

<Just work stuff. Nothing for you to worry about.>

Eleanor didn't believe her, and her mom had never kept stuff from her. <When will you be able to text again?>

<Soon, I hope.>

<You hope?>

<Soon, I said. Soon.>

That did not comfort Eleanor. <Fine>

<Say hi to Uncle Jack for me.>

<I will.>

22

<I love you, sweetie. So much.>

<love you too>

<Good-bye>

<bye>

And that was it. The connection between them went cold.

— CHAPTER —
3

I T HAD SNOWED A BIT DURING THE NIGHT, A FINE, DRY DUST
that looked like someone had shaken a bag of flour
over the city. The sunlight fell sharply against it. Eleanor took the walk to school warm inside her inner
and outer coats, mittens, and the hat her mother had
bought her before she'd left for the Arctic. It was an
old-style leather aviator cap, lined with fur, with flaps
over her ears. As she walked, Eleanor went back over
the texts from last night in her mind. She'd stayed up
late worrying about what it was her mom was keeping
from her, trying to puzzle it out. Did it have something to do with her mother's expedition onto the ice
sheet? But now, with the clarity of the fresh morning,

Eleanor had begun to wonder if she was worrying about nothing.

She approached the Ice Castles and found Jenna and Claire waiting outside their building for Eleanor like they usually did, bobbing a little in the cold. It was her first time seeing them since they'd all been hauled into the police station, and Eleanor didn't quite know what to expect. She hadn't even been sure they'd wait for her.

"Hey," Eleanor said when she reached them.

"Hey," they said.

The three of them formed a little circle, huddled around the cloud of their mingled breath.

"So . . ." Eleanor swept a trail through the snow dust with the side of her boot. "Did you guys get in trouble?"

"A little," Jenna said. "But my mom believed me when I told her I got tricked into it."

"Me too," said Claire. "At this point, my parents really don't like you, Ellie."

Eleanor shrugged. "That has already been duly noted. But are *you* guys still mad at me?"

"I was," said Jenna. "But I'm not anymore."

"Me neither," said Claire.

"Good," Eleanor said. "Okay."

"Okay. Can we get to school now?" Jenna bobbed

again. "They rationed the heat in the Ice Castles last night, and I am so cold. I just want to get warm."

"Rationed the heat?" Eleanor said. "Why?"

"Energy shortage, I guess," Claire said.

An energy shortage if you're poor or a refugee. Eleanor huffed. This was exactly why her mother was doing what she was doing up in the Arctic. They needed to find enough oil to keep *everyone* warm, not just those with money. "I'm so sorry," she said.

Claire just shook her head. "It's okay. Can we—? Let's just go."

"Of course," Eleanor said.

They set off at a brisk pace. Eleanor felt bad but didn't know what to say. It wasn't just what people could afford to throw away, like Uncle Jack had said, that told you how rich they were. It was also what people took for granted. Those who lived in the mansions where Uncle Jack worked took their apples and bananas for granted. Eleanor took her heat for granted. And as bad as the Ice Castles were, refugees who got turned away would probably say that the people who lived there were lucky, too.

"What do you guys have first period, again?" Jenna asked.

"Science," Claire said.

"I hate science," Eleanor said, grateful for a change

26

in subject. But her mom paid more attention to her science and math grades than anything else. Eleanor liked English class. She liked the novels, the stories about the earth before the Freeze, a world where people as far north as Canada could go swimming in lakes and rivers that hadn't frozen over. She liked to read about warmth and could almost feel it emanating from the pages. It was like reading fantasy or science fiction.

They made their way through the cold streets to the school. The plastic construction sheet still covered the new wing. At the sight of it, Eleanor grinned to herself—*devilishly clever*—and went inside.

Science class was in the gym, along with an eighth-grade math class and a seventh-grade social studies class. The classrooms weren't big enough to hold all the students anymore. It was loud, and a line of neon tape was all that separated one class from another. Eleanor wanted to sit on the back bleachers, but Claire dragged her up to the third row, where they had the best chance of actually hearing the teacher.

Mr. Fiske wore a skinny black tie today, sleeves rolled up on his white shirt, and jeans. He stood on the floor of the gym next to a projector and a screen, which was a little hard to see without dimming the lights. He held his right hand over his head, and it looked like he might have been snapping his fingers. Eleanor couldn't tell, and certainly couldn't hear it.

"Ladies and gentlemen!" he shouted.

Eleanor craned her neck toward him. The guy teaching the math class next to them was also the coach of the football team, and his lesson on exponents carried over everything.

"Today," Mr. Fiske said, "we begin our climate unit."

A collective groan issued from the bleachers, but Eleanor was pretty sure that sound would have been the same for any subject, and unlike seemingly every other person in the class, including Claire, Eleanor didn't mind the idea of a climate unit.

"We'll begin with the Milankovitch-Skinner Cycles. Does anyone know what they are?"

No hands went up.

Mr. Fiske nodded. "Okay, then. In the first half of the twentieth century, Dr. Milankovitch theorized that the shape of the earth's orbit around the sun, and the tilt and rotation of its axis, affected the climate." The screen switched to a video of the earth careening around the solar system. "His calculations produced a predictable cycle of glacial ages. But apparently, his calculations were wrong. We weren't supposed to enter another ice age for fifty thousand years. But in the early part of the twenty-first century, a young graduate student discovered something." Mr. Fiske switched the screen to the photo of a man everyone on the planet knew: Dr. Skinner, the renowned climatologist, now CEO of the Global Energy Trust, one of the largest oil and energy companies in the world. "Aaron Skinner demonstrated that our climate was changing sooner than expected, and another ice age was upon us."

Eleanor had actually met Dr. Skinner at a big oil company conference with her mom. He was just as good-looking in person.

"At first," Mr. Fiske said, "his warnings went unheeded by both the government and the scientific community." The screen changed to newspaper headlines and photos. Shriveled crops ruined by frost in August. Forlorn beachfront houses now sitting a half mile from the ocean. Scores of people killed in freak blizzards. "But soon the world realized that Dr. Skinner had been right. Our whole world was changing."

Eleanor had never known a different world. But her mom and Uncle Jack could still remember what it was like before.

Mr. Fiske had paused in his lesson, probably for some kind of dramatic effect. "Dr. Skinner recalculated Milankovitch's orbital cycles and proved that we have entered a new ice age, right on schedule. And now, it's up to all of us to work together to—"

Eleanor's bag chimed. She heard it over Mr. Fiske's lecture, which kept droning on. It cut through the booming voice of the math teacher next door, and through the student chatter all around her. It was her Sync.

She whipped it out. The screen flashed a text message.

<Hi, sweetie. I just wanted to apologize for cutting you off so abruptly last night. We're about to head out, so I still don't have time to talk, but I just wanted to tell you not to worry, because I know you are. ;) I'll be in touch soon. I love you. Mom >

Being told not to worry was almost guaranteed to make Eleanor worry even more. Something still felt off. It wasn't what her mom was saying. It was what she *wasn't* saying. She always told Eleanor everything, even the boring science stuff, details about ice cores and carbon levels and all that.

Claire was leaning toward her, obviously trying to read the message out of the corner of her eye, so Eleanor just turned the screen toward her and let her see it directly.

A moment later, Claire looked up from the screen and smiled. Then she whispered in Eleanor's ear, "That's good, right?"

"No, it's not," Eleanor whispered back.

"Why not?"

"I don't know. It just isn't."

"Well, it sounds good to me. I wish my mom would send me a text like that, and she's only a few miles away, waiting for food rations."

That shifted Eleanor's perspective a bit. At least her family didn't have to wait in those terrible lines. She typed a return message, hoping her mom might get it before she headed out onto the ice sheet.

<Thanks, Mom. It's okay, I know you're busy. Talk soon. Be safe. Love you.>

Claire had read the reply over Eleanor's shoulder and nodded her approval. The moment after sending it, Eleanor felt a bit better. She sighed as she slipped the Sync into her bag and turned her attention back to the lecture.

". . . current glaciation," Mr. Fiske said. The screen showed a spatchcocked map of the world. "As you can see, the ice sheet has completely covered the northern half of the United States, stretching from Oregon to Washington, DC. In places, the ice reaches a depth of three kilometers—almost two miles." The screen switched to an image of Europe. "The UK is almost completely covered in ice, as you can see, along with most of northern Europe."

31

A student up at the front raised his hand. "How far south will the ice go?"

Mr. Fiske inhaled. "That depends on where you are. The ice behaves differently in Asia, for example, where glaciation is not as extensive. Here in the US, the ice sheet is still advancing at a rate of .8 meters per day, or about 2.7 feet. That is a slower pace than has been seen in the last ten years, so scientists are hopeful the advance is slowing."

"But . . . ," the student said, "how far will it go?"

Eleanor knew what he was really asking. He wanted to know if the ice would one day reach Phoenix. He wanted to know if the ice would ever stop. Or would it keep on clawing and pressing down on them, eventually covering the whole world? It was a question every person on earth asked. It hung in the air like the cold, always there, even when Eleanor tried to ignore it, chilling her thoughts.

Last night they'd rationed heat to the Ice Castles. One day, would they ration heat to the whole city? The country? The world?

Mr. Fiske paused this time, as though he were reluctant to answer. "I'm afraid we still don't know."

A hush followed, and then a moment later the students' voices swelled to a murmur.

"But . . . ," Mr. Fiske said loudly, waving his index

finger at the ceiling, "we have something no other species in the history of the planet has ever had." He brought the index finger down and laid it against his temple. "Our brain. The human mind is an ingenious thing, and we will find a way to survive in an age when so many other animals go extinct. Companies like the G.E.T. have put the smartest men and women in the world to work"—Eleanor tuned in more intently at the mention of the G.E.T.—"and their mission is to make sure we have the energy we need."

He paused again with a slight frown. "Of course, they're also one of the largest corporations on the planet, and because of that, there are those who mistrust them. In today's economy, some believe energy to be a basic human right. They do not believe *any* company should profit from it."

Eleanor's mother had come to that conclusion a long time ago, which was why she took a smaller salary and worked for a nonprofit.

Mr. Fiske continued. "Others would argue the G.E.T. have *earned* financial compensation for their innovation and investment in our future." He spread his hands wide. "Consider all they've done—"

"Then why don't they disclose their earnings?" some kid asked from the front.

"Well," Mr. Fiske said, "they have an agreement

33

with the UN Security Council that—"

"I know that," the kid said, "but *why?*"

Eleanor's mother had wondered the same thing.

"Mr. Fiske," the kid said, "have you ever heard of the Preservation Protocol?"

Eleanor had heard of it, in a boogeyman kind of way. It was supposedly a plan the UN had come up with to decide which countries would get energy, and which wouldn't, if the ice sheet never stopped.

"I've heard of it." Mr. Fiske just stood there a moment, looking at the kid. "But like most rational people, I regard it as the unfounded conspiracy theory it is. The G.E.T. is a *company*, not some secret society. And this is a science class. The politics of global energy are outside our purview. Let's get back on track."

Eleanor slumped down lower onto the bleacher. Mr. Fiske had moved on, lecturing on prehistoric ice ages, but something about his exchange with that student bothered her. Her mom was up in the Arctic, risking her life, going out onto the ice sheet and who knows what else, because of what she believed in, and Eleanor had to believe her work wasn't in vain.

She got through the rest of the school day, checking her Sync several times in case she'd missed the chime. No messages. She walked home with Claire and Jenna and said good-bye to them at the Ice Castles, telling them she hoped the city wouldn't be rationing energy again that night.

At home, she helped Uncle Jack cook a mushroom risotto for dinner and couldn't help feeling a little guilty with each delicious bite. Afterward, they got out the chessboard, but her head wasn't really in the game.

"Admit it," Uncle Jack said. "You're letting me win."

He knew what was on her mind and was trying to lighten the mood. "It's the only way you can win," she said with mock sincerity. "And I just feel so bad for you."

"How sportsmanlike."

She closed her eyes. "I know. You're welcome."

"Eleanor, I—"

The chime of the Sync cut him off.

— CHAPTER —
4

THE MESSAGE MADE NO SENSE. IT WASN'T EVEN REALLY A message, it was just a batch of files. Eleanor opened them, one by one, hoping to find something to help her make sense of what her mom was sending her. But all she found were diagrams that she recognized from her science class as star charts, with lines and equations drawn across them in sweeping arcs. There were maps of the world with crisscrossing lines connecting far-flung locations, wrapping the globe in a spiderweb. There were pages and pages of mathematical equations.

"What is this?" Eleanor asked out loud, sitting alone in her room on her bed.

The images all had a watermark in the bottom-right corner.

G.E.T.

Never mind what the files were—what was her mom doing with them?

The Sync chimed again, and a new batch of files came in, as incomprehensible as the first. One of them appeared to be an Arctic map showing the city of Barrow, Alaska, as well as the research station where her mom must be currently stationed, inside the National Petroleum Reserve. More pages of equations, charts, and graphs. This batch didn't have the G.E.T. watermark.

The Sync chimed a third time, and a text came through.

    <Eleanor, you must keep all this safe. Keep it secret. I will contact you when I can. I love you, sweetie. So much.>

Eleanor typed quickly. <mom are you ok>

   . . .

<mom>

   . . .

<mom answer me>

   . . .

Eleanor waited. No reply came through. She didn't

know what all these files meant, but she intended to do with them exactly what her mother asked her to do.

Uncle Jack knocked on the door and came in. "Everything okay, Ell Bell?"

When her mom said "secret," Eleanor didn't think she meant from Uncle Jack. "Mom sent me a bunch of files. Maps and stuff." She then read the text to him.

"That's weird," Uncle Jack said.

"Yeah." All this only fed Eleanor's earlier worries. "I knew there was something going on she wasn't telling me."

"She mentioned her company had partnered with the G.E.T. on an energy project."

"She did?"

"Before she left on this trip."

Eleanor looked at the blank screen of her Sync. "But she hates the G.E.T."

"She doesn't hate them, Ellie, she just doesn't agree with them. Her team discovered something they didn't have the resources to pursue. Some kind of massive oil deposit or something. The G.E.T. came in to help."

"She's working for them?"

"Working *with* them. Temporarily."

"So why is she sending me this stuff?"

Uncle Jack palmed his head with his thick hand and rubbed his hair. "I don't know."

"It's not all G.E.T. stuff. Only the first batch was. This other stuff is hers." Eleanor looked up at the ceiling, at the Spackle where she used to see animals and faces. "It sounds like she's in some kind of trouble."

"I'm sure she's fine, Ell Bell." Uncle Jack sat down next to her, and the bed squealed. "It sounds like things are really tense for her right now. Super busy. But I'm sure she's fine."

Eleanor wasn't sure.

"Try to put it out of your mind for now, okay? Maybe get to bed?" He rubbed her back. "Hopefully, she'll be in touch tomorrow and you can find out what all this means."

Eleanor didn't know how she'd get to sleep, but she nodded. Uncle Jack leaned over, kissed the top of her head, and left the room. She dressed for bed and brushed her teeth, and as she closed her bedroom door, she called downstairs, "Good night, Uncle Jack. Love you."

"Love you, Ell Bell. Night."

Eleanor climbed into bed. She tried to fall asleep but couldn't stop the thoughts barreling toward her. Her mom was working with the G.E.T., and she hadn't said anything about it. Eleanor felt a bit betrayed. But her disappointment at that was overshadowed by her fear. She imagined her mom, lost and alone at the top of the world, stumbling away from her across a wasteland of ice, a desolate emptiness beating at her from all sides. A fierce wind tore at her, dissolving her in the distance, swallowing her up into the white void.

Eleanor clamped her eyes shut and shook her head. It couldn't be. It just couldn't be. Her mom was fine, just like Uncle Jack said. But she pulled up her Sync.

<mom?>

. . .

She waited. <mom?>

. . .

<just tell me you're ok. please.>

. . .

She fought back tears. <please mom>

. . .

<mom>

. . .

Something rang in the middle of the night. Eleanor shot awake and grabbed her Sync but realized, staring at the blank screen, it'd been the sound of a phone. Uncle Jack's phone down in the living room. He always slept on the couch, refusing to use Eleanor's mother's room. Eleanor crept from her bed and opened her door just a crack, wide enough to listen. In the silence of the house, she could hear his hushed voice murmuring up the stairs.

"Yes, this is him. . . . Okay. . . . Oh no. . . . Is she—I see. . . . So when was the last time—? . . . Uh-huh."

It was about her mom. Eleanor knew it. She bolted from her room, down the stairs, into the living room.

Uncle Jack looked up as she came in but held his index finger to his lips. "So what's the next step?" he said.

"What is it?" Eleanor whispered.

Uncle Jack ignored her. "Yes, she's here with me now. I can tell her."

Eleanor leaned in, her whole body trembling. "Tell me what?"

Uncle Jack held up the palm of his hand to silence her. "Yes, she has it. . . . Okay. Okay, that sounds good. Thank you for the call. Please keep me updated the minute you know more. . . . Thank you."

The second he hung up, Eleanor raised her voice. "Uncle Jack, what—?"

"Eleanor, I will explain, but I need you to—"

"Just tell me!"

"I'm trying, but you need to stay calm. You need to listen carefully. Okay?"

41

She backed up from him and settled her shaking as best she could. "Okay."

"Okay." He took a deep breath. "Now. The expedition your mother took onto the ice sheet has not returned."

"She's LOST?"

"No, listen. They've lost contact is all. She's probably fine, but they wanted to keep us informed."

"She's lost on the ice sheet!" Eleanor couldn't stop the shaking now. Her breathing and her voice turned frantic. "How can she be fine?"

"She texted you, didn't she? She and her partner have food and equipment. They know how to survive on the ice. The G.E.T. is searching for them. They'll find her, but they need your help."

"What, what can I— We can go up there! We can help search!"

"We're not going to the Arctic," he said. "They just need your Sync. They can use it to help locate your mom. The G.E.T. is sending someone to pick it up in the morning."

Eleanor stopped shaking. Her body went cold. "They want my Sync?"

"Yes."

An alarm blared at the back of her mind. "They can't take my Sync."

"Eleanor, if it will help find her—"

"No. It's the only way I have to contact her. Or for her to contact me." She wasn't giving that up to anyone.

"Eleanor, this isn't a choice. Now go get it for me."

Eleanor shook her head. "I won't." And then she remembered the files and the message her mother had sent. Her mom had entrusted all that to Eleanor, and Eleanor had to keep it safe, even from the G.E.T. Maybe even especially from the G.E.T. No matter what happened, Eleanor knew she wasn't giving up her Sync until she heard from her mom. She folded her arms. "I won't give it to them," she said.

"Eleanor, please. Please don't do this." Uncle Jack let out a sigh that carried the weight of everything Eleanor had put him through. "Please. You don't— I can't— Just bring me the Sync, okay?"

"No, Uncle Jack, I—"

"PLEASE!" he shouted.

Eleanor flinched. She'd never heard him raise his voice before. Most other parents would have lost it after the police station, or well before, but not Uncle Jack. The outburst stunned her protests into silence.

"I'm sorry." He held up both hands. "Eleanor, listen to me carefully. I know this is hard for you. It's hard for me, too. The world is a hard place, and it keeps getting harder. It's not what any of us wanted. But we need to do whatever we can to bring your mom home."

Eleanor kept her voice calm. She didn't want to upset Uncle Jack any further. She didn't want to be the one who made him yell. He had been so kind to her, and she knew how scared he must be. He was responsible for Eleanor if something happened to her mom.

"I'm sorry, Uncle Jack." She took hold of both his hands. "But my mom sent me that stuff for a reason. Don't you think it's weird that as soon as she sent it, the G.E.T. wants to come and take my Sync?"

"Eleanor, sweetie," Uncle Jack began. "Think about it. It also makes sense that the G.E.T. could use it to find her."

"Is there anyone else you could call to find out what's going on? Someone Mom trusts?"

Uncle Jack wrinkled his lips into a sideways frown. "The research station used to have a satellite phone. Before they started using the Syncs. They may still have it."

"Could you call it?"

"I can try."

Eleanor watched as he scrolled through the contacts on his phone and dialed. She waited as he held the phone to his ear, head bowed.

"Good, it's ringing," he said. A moment later, he

looked up. Eleanor could hear that someone had answered. "Yes, hello," he said. "This is Jack Perry, Dr. Perry's brother. Who is this? . . . Dr. Grant, hi. . . . Yes, that's why I'm calling. Do you—?"

This time, Eleanor forced herself to wait until he'd finished the conversation before she asked him any questions.

"I see," Uncle Jack said. "Yes, that's what we were told. . . . Uh-huh. Okay, I would really appreciate that. You have my number now. Thanks, Dr. Grant." He hung up.

"Who was that?" Eleanor asked. "What did he say?"

"That was an old colleague of your mom's. I've met him—he's a nice guy. He said the same thing. They've lost contact with your mom and they're searching for her."

Eleanor realized she'd let herself hope that the first call was somehow a mistake, but she couldn't deny anymore that her mom was in serious danger. Nothing could live on the Arctic ice sheet, where temperatures could drop a hundred degrees below zero and colder. That was enough to kill most living things within minutes unless they had serious protection. To think of her mom lost out there overwhelmed Eleanor to the point of tears.

"We have to do something," she said.

"We can, Ell Bell. They need your Sync."

Maybe he was right. After all, what was more important? Those files, or her mother's life? She nodded. "I'll go get it for you."

She turned to go upstairs, but he reached out and pulled her into one of his huge, protective hugs. She hugged him back and felt him trembling, so slightly she almost couldn't detect it. But it was there.

"Tell you what," he said. "You keep it until tomorrow morning, okay? Keep it safe until the G.E.T. arrives."

She squeezed him more tightly. "Thanks."

He let her go and turned away, wiping his eyes. Eleanor left him and went upstairs. She climbed back into bed with the Sync and clutched it to her chest. The earlier, nameless fears had become very real, which meant that she could argue with them now. She reminded herself that her mom had extensive training in how to stay alive out on the ice. She had equipment and supplies. She could survive. She *had* to survive.

As the night passed without sleep, time stretched and bounced back, minutes and hours seeming to change places, throwing Eleanor into a hazy disorientation. Her eyes closed and fluttered open, again and again. Never quite awake, never quite asleep. She didn't know how long she lay there. Morning had not yet begun to enter the room, but she felt it on the horizon. She couldn't go to school that day. Not with—

The Sync chimed against her chest, muffled.

Eleanor jolted upright, fumbling it into view.

<70 56 28 24 156 53 27 80 SHOW NO ONE. I will c>

Eleanor typed as quickly as she could. <mom are you ok where are you>

. . .

<MOM>

. . .

<mom tell me where you are ARE YOU OK>

. . .

Why didn't her mom answer? She had just sent a text. Was she hurt? Freezing to death? Then it occurred to Eleanor.

The battery.

If her mom was stranded out on the ice sheet, she might be trying to conserve the power left in her Sync. Maybe that was why her last message seemed cut off. Maybe the battery had finally died.

There wasn't any way for Eleanor to know, but what she *did* know was that her mom had just sent her another warning. *Show no one.* There wasn't any way she would let the G.E.T. take her Sync. Not now.

She had no idea what the numbers in the message could mean. Were they some kind of code? A password, maybe? Eleanor needed more information, but she didn't need to know what the numbers meant to know her mom was in serious trouble. Maybe she was trapped, or injured. Eleanor got out of bed and went for the door. She had to show Uncle Jack—

She stopped.

The first messages had demanded secrecy, too, but Uncle Jack hadn't cared about that. Even if Eleanor showed him this message, he would still turn the Sync and the numbers over to the G.E.T., which Eleanor knew was exactly what her mother *didn't* want. The numbers were intended for Eleanor, and it was up to Eleanor to find out what they meant. It was up to her to go and find her mom. The G.E.T. would arrive in a matter of hours for the Sync.

Eleanor knew she had to be gone well before then.

CHAPTER 5

THERE WERE NO PASSENGER FLIGHTS HEADING NORTH. The only people who flew north were oil company workers, oil prospectors, and the cargo planes that supplied them, and not all those flights were exactly legal. If she was going to go searching for her mom, Eleanor knew she'd have to buy or bribe her way onto one of the cargo planes. Her mom kept emergency money rolled up in a quart-size mason jar at the back of her closet. Most people kept money on hand these days, as a precaution—banks and economies in other countries had been collapsing—and her mom had stashed away about two thousand dollars. Eleanor took all that money, and as quietly as she could, she packed everything she thought she might need, pillaging her mom's supply of spare equipment and gear. Thermal underwear with nanoheaters woven into the fabric. Coats, gloves, and goggles. Boots and the metal-toothed crampons to strap onto their soles if she needed them. A hermetic sleeping bag. A face mask that warmed up the air before it hit your lungs—

The sight of the mask stopped her. The *need* for it stopped her. What was she doing, going to a place where her own unaided breathing could freeze her from the inside out?

She shook her head and zipped that thought away with all the equipment inside her mom's old pack. All she needed to worry about right now was getting on a flight. She slipped out of the bedroom and down the stairs. In the darkness of the living room, she watched the rise and fall of Uncle Jack's bulk on the couch, making sure he was asleep.

Poor Uncle Jack.

She hoped he would forgive her. She eased the front door open, squeezed through, and then eased it closed again, all without waking him.

Out on the sidewalk, she slung the pack up onto her back, and it was a lot heavier than she'd been expecting. She almost lost her balance, but she wiggled under the straps and adjusted herself to the weight of it.

The reluctant sun still huddled over the horizon, but its first soft glow had arrived. Eleanor pulled out a bus map she'd printed, the routes to the airfield highlighted, and walked to her first stop.

The schedule didn't have the next bus leaving for seventeen minutes. As she stood waiting there for it, the early-morning cold closed in. She wasn't normally outside at this time. Few people were unless they had to be. Eleanor hadn't worn her warmest gear. She didn't think she'd need it until she reached the Arctic, but now she wished she'd put it all on. It only took a few moments for her teeth to start chattering, her fingers and toes to tingle, her nose and ears to hurt.

Before her mom's first Arctic trip, she had gone over the effects of cold on the human body with Eleanor. It had probably been a misguided, overly intellectual attempt to alleviate some of Eleanor's fears. It hadn't worked.

When facing extreme cold, the human body immediately reroutes blood to vital organs, leaving the extremities without adequate circulation and vulnerable to frostbite. This has other effects, like going numb, and the increased blood supply to the kidneys makes you have to pee. Metabolism slows to conserve energy, which in turn slows brain activity, making you feel sluggish and foggy. The cold makes you stupid.

But these are only delay tactics. It's all just the body's effort to save what it can, the most important organs, until you're able to get somewhere warm. Because the human body is not meant to survive in cold like this. It can't.

Without normal blood supply, your legs and arms get weaker and weaker, making it harder to move. Skin cells start to rupture, and tissue dies. The numbness and the fogginess only get worse until you start to think it would be a good idea to lie down and take a nap. That's when the cold finally wins.

And that's the thing. The cold *always* wins. All it needs is time.

Eleanor wasn't at the point of lying down on the sidewalk just yet, but if she felt this cold right now, here in Phoenix, how would it be in the Arctic?

The bus rumbled up a few minutes later. Eleanor stamped her feet and leaped on board as soon as the doors hissed open.

Eleanor had to change buses at the city's main terminal. She disembarked at the same time a new batch of refugees unloaded just up the curb, their eyes glassy from exhaustion and disbelief. Everything they owned they carried in suitcases and duffel bags, having left the rest behind for the ice to devour. Government workers walked among them, giving instructions, handing them slips of paper with their new addresses in the Ice Castles. Their new homes.

Eleanor wondered where they had come from. Idaho? Wyoming? What had their lives been like, with the ice sheet bearing down on them, grinding everything underfoot? How long had they clung to their homes before surrendering it all to the ice and retreating? How hard had it been to make that decision?

When Eleanor thought about having to do the same, she knew the decision would be an easy one. She wasn't attached to her house, or to Phoenix. Even though she'd lived there most of her life, she'd never felt like she belonged. Her mom and Uncle Jack, they were her home. When it came time for Eleanor to hang on to something, to refuse to give ground to the ice, that was where she would make her stand. That was why she was going north.

She turned away from the refugees and found her next bus, climbed aboard, and a short ride later, she arrived at the city's general aviation airfield. Phoenix's Sky Harbor airport still ran nearby. Eleanor could see its terminal and flight tower in the distance across the tarmac. But the planes over there carried only travelers heading south. The airlines rarely ever sent a passenger flight north.

Eleanor's only chance would be here, and she had to get on a plane soon. The tremulous sun had just crested the horizon. Uncle Jack would be awake soon. He'd probably assume Eleanor was asleep in her bed and let her be for a little while. But not for long. Eleanor had no idea when the G.E.T. would show up for her Sync, but she planned to be in the air with it heading north before then.

Cargo planes of all sizes sat on the tarmac, maintenance crews scrambling over and around them, tanker trucks with antifreeze hosing them down, guys with Ping-Pong paddles directing pilots for takeoff from the ground. There were lots of large buildings and hangars squatting in clusters. Windowless, industrial structures, muted paint fading and peeling.

Eleanor realized she had no idea where to go or how to go about this. She needed a pilot heading to Barrow, ideally. But failing that, a pilot at least flying to Alaska. She figured the chances of that were good, since Alaska had become a hub for oil dealing in North America, and that was where most of the supply-laden northbound flights would be headed.

But what should she do? Just go up and ask someone? *Hey, I don't suppose you'd mind taking a twelve-year-old girl on your plane?*

The other problem was the fence. There was only

one gate she could see onto the airfield, where vehicles were checked, and Eleanor was pretty sure the security guards working there wouldn't just let her through. But she adjusted her pack and walked toward it, trying to keep her head up, like she knew exactly where she was going.

As she approached, she noticed what looked like a big red shed with a white metal roof just a bit down the road from the gate on her side of the fence, a few trucks and other vehicles parked in front of it. A stenciled sign above the door read PROP STOP CAFE. Eleanor didn't know what a "prop stop" was, but it sounded like it might be a plane thing, and if the café had that kind of name, it might be the kind of place pilots hung out. Maybe she could talk to someone in there about flying north.

The building looked like a shed on the inside, too, with rough wooden walls and floor. But it was warm and clean, and it smelled of bacon and butter. Eleanor had left her home that morning without eating breakfast and felt suddenly hungry.

There were several men and women at the tables, some of them wearing regular coats, some of them wearing the utility gear she'd seen on the ground crews out on the tarmac, all of them a bit rough-looking. She didn't see any waiters or waitresses, though. Just a window back into the kitchen, where a large man with a yellow bandanna tied around his head hunched over a steaming griddle.

"Feel free to seat yourself!" he called to Eleanor over his shoulder.

The men and women she passed stared at her as she sought out an empty booth and took a seat, setting her pack on the floor. Were any of these people pilots? What should she do, stand up and make an announcement? Go around the room whispering? She needed to know which, if any of them, were going to the Arctic, and which would be willing to take her.

"What can I get you?"

Eleanor glanced toward the kitchen window. The cook leaned through it, gripping the ledge, looking at her.

"Um. Scrambled eggs?"

"Bacon or sausage?"

"Sausage."

"Adam and Eve on a log and wreck 'em!" he shouted before disappearing.

Adam and Eve? Who is he talking to?

Two men seated at a nearby table were watching her. Eyeing her pack. She pulled it closer and felt the first twinge of nervousness since she'd left home earlier that morning. She didn't know who these people were, where they were from, or where they were going. How could she trust any of them?

A small TV was perched high in one of the corners, tuned to a news station. Eleanor couldn't really hear what the reporter was saying, but it was one of those UN meetings where no one looked like they were actually listening to the woman speaking. Headlines scrolled across the bottom of the screen.

MEXICAN PRESIDENT SANCHEZ PLEDGES BILLIONS IN ADDITIONAL AID TO THE UNITED STATES. . . .

THE GLOBAL ENERGY TRUST ASSUMES CONTROL OF THE ARABIAN PENINSULA'S OIL RESERVES. VIOLENT PROTESTS ERUPT ACROSS THE MIDDLE EAST. . . .

SCIENTISTS ESTIMATE THAT FEWER THAN ONE HUNDRED AFRICAN LIONS REMAIN IN THE WILD DUE TO LAND DEVELOPERS—

"Order up!" The cook tapped a bell, set Eleanor's food in the window, and disappeared. Eleanor still hadn't seen a waiter or waitress.

"You gotta go get it," one of the two men said. "Kimball's a one-man show."

"Oh." Eleanor stood, looked at her pack, looked at

the men, then hurried to the window for her plate. She doused her eggs with a splash of Tabasco before digging in. They weren't as fluffy and creamy as Uncle Jack's.

"So, uh . . ." The man who'd told her to get her food leaned toward her. "Your dad work on the airfield or something?"

"Nope." Eleanor stabbed a sausage link with a fork and bit off half of it. "Just felt like some eggs."

He leaned back. "Uh-huh. Sure you did."

"Traveling?" asked the other guy. He wore a camo-print ball cap.

"Are you?" Eleanor asked.

"Always," camo guy said.

"Are you a pilot?" Eleanor asked.

"We both are," he said, gesturing to the first guy. "Where are you headed?"

"I didn't say I was headed anywhere," Eleanor said.

"No, ma'am, you didn't. But Kimball sure ain't known for his eggs and sausage. His hash, on the other hand—"

"I'm not heading anywhere." Eleanor made her voice firm. She had started to think that the kind of pilots who *would* take a twelve-year-old girl north were the exact pilots she should avoid. Some of the stories she'd heard about the Arctic replayed in her mind.

There wasn't much of a government left up there, no law, just a loose community of drillers.

"It's okay." Camo hat reached out his hand and laid it on Eleanor's table. "You're not the first runaway to come through here. Not by a long shot. Depending on what you're offering, maybe we can help you out. Where do you wanna go? Vegas? Houston?"

Okay, now this guy was really creeping Eleanor out. "Barrow," she said with sarcastic emphasis. "Alaska."

"Ha!" The first guy laughed. "You're funny, kid."

She shrugged.

Camo hat wasn't smiling. He pulled his hand back. "Suit yourself. Your problems are your problems. Just trying to help."

Sure he was. Eleanor knew she wasn't getting on a plane with either of these guys, but maybe they could still be useful. "What's wrong?" She kept the sarcasm in her voice. "You don't fly up to Alaska? Is your plane too . . . small?"

"Ha!" The first guy laughed again and slapped the table.

"My plane is just fine," camo hat said, grinning now. "But if that's really where you're heading, you're out of luck. There aren't a lot of planes going that far north these days."

Eleanor hoped that wasn't true. But now it was

time to bluff. "Well, I know a pilot who's here right now, and he goes up there all the time."

"Who?" camo hat said. "Luke?"

Luke.

"Yeah," she said. "Luke."

"Luke." The first guy kind of growled a little and shook his head. "I'd be flying up there all the time, too, if I had his fat contracts."

"Have you seen him around?" Eleanor asked.

"Yeah, he's parked in hangar eighteen today," camo hat said.

"Thanks." Eleanor left some of the money from her mom's stash on the table to pay for her breakfast. "Later, guys." She gathered her pack and left the café.

Outside, she looked at the line of parked vehicles. One of them, a big utility truck, had an airport label and service number painted on its doors. Eleanor bet that one was headed through the gate. She glanced around to make sure no one was looking and then climbed up into the truck bed. There wasn't much back there to conceal her. Just some big blue plastic barrels she wedged herself between. After she'd hunkered down, she craned her neck and was pretty sure she'd be hidden from the view of the driver where she was. Her only hope was that the security guards wouldn't really scrutinize the truck bed at the gate.

Minutes went by. Eleanor felt the cold of the morning seeping in again, and she hoped the driver of this truck wouldn't take forever eating his or her breakfast.

More minutes passed. Eleanor's teeth started chattering. She wondered if Uncle Jack had noticed she was gone yet. She wondered if the G.E.T. had come for the Sync. Were they already out looking for her?

She was about to pull out her Sync to check the time when she heard the truck door open and felt the bed teeter slightly beneath her feet as the driver climbed in. The door closed, and the engine started.

This is it.

The truck eased backward from the café into the street, its pungent exhaust rolling over Eleanor, burning her eyes and nose. Then it pulled forward, and Eleanor tried to make herself as small as she could. The bumps in the road sloshed the liquid contents inside the barrels next to her ears. A few moments later, the truck slowed down and came to a stop. They were at the gate. Eleanor closed her eyes as a male voice carried back to her.

"Good morning," he said, sounding bored. "Badge?" That had to be the security guard.

"Morning," a woman said. Eleanor assumed she was the driver. "Long night?"

"Yep. But my shift ends in fifteen."

"Wish I could say the same."

A moment went by. "Thank you," the man said. "Proceed through the gate."

The truck pulled ahead, but Eleanor didn't let herself breathe until it had driven well past the gate. The driver took a winding route between the airfield's buildings. Eleanor tried to keep track of the turns but soon became disoriented and gave up. A few minutes later, the truck came to a stop, and the driver turned off the engine. Eleanor heard the door open, then close. She waited several moments, long enough for the driver to have gone, and then got up, put her pack on, and leaped down out of the truck bed.

"Hey!" The woman stood a short distance off, smoking a cigarette. "What are you—?"

Eleanor didn't wait to hear what she was going to say. She ran.

— CHAPTER —
6

"HEY!" THE DRIVER SHOUTED.

Eleanor's pack bounced hard against her back. She dove into the narrow alleyway between two buildings, elbows grazing either side. She didn't know if the driver was chasing her, but she didn't even turn to look.

Eleanor burst out from between the buildings into a wider road. She threw herself down another narrow alleyway, across an even wider road, and into an open, dark hangar, where she crouched down in the shadows, slowed her breathing, and listened.

She didn't hear anyone coming. But she heard indistinct shouting. It sounded like a few people were calling back and forth about her. They knew she was here, somewhere on the airfield, and they were looking for her. If she got caught, this would be way worse than being reprimanded at the police station. She'd get arrested for sure. They'd call Uncle Jack, he'd take her Sync, and Eleanor would lose any hope she had of finding her mom.

Her only chance was to get to hangar eighteen and somehow bribe her way onto this Luke guy's plane before anyone caught her.

Eleanor waited a few minutes longer, trying to figure out if the voices were coming closer. When she felt pretty sure they weren't, she crept forward and peeked out of the hangar. The road outside was lined with buildings, but like the one in which she now hid, none of them seemed large enough. She assumed Luke's plane would have to be pretty big to make his Arctic runs.

Farther down the road, the buildings doubled and tripled in size. She decided to make her way toward them. Fortunately, it was still pretty early in the morning, and the road appeared deserted in both directions.

Eleanor scurried out but kept to the sides of the road off the pavement, running like a mouse in a corner, close to the buildings, her boots leaving footprints in the sand and snow. She'd made it a block or so when she heard the sound of an engine approaching.

She ducked down behind a stack of empty wooden pallets, peering through the splintered slats as a utility truck rounded a corner up ahead and turned in the same direction she was headed, toward the larger hangars. She watched it drive off, getting smaller, until it turned another corner and disappeared.

She waited a few more seconds before continuing down the road. On the way, she hid from two more trucks, as well as a group of guys wearing those big headset things around their necks, until she reached the first of the large buildings.

Through a window in back, she could see it was a hangar, but it was empty. She moved on to the next, which had two smaller, sleek planes inside it, not what she was looking for.

"Can I help you?"

Eleanor whipped around.

A young guy stood there, a coil of hose over his shoulder that almost reached the ground. Eleanor thought about running again, but this guy didn't seem like he was after her, or cared who she was.

"I'm, uh, looking for hangar eighteen," she said.

"Two more down." He pointed. "That way."

"Thank you." She nodded and walked on, forcing herself to move slowly and openly.

Security on this side of the airfield seemed a lot looser than it was in the passenger airport. No alarms here. Maybe that was all part of the deal. Maybe all the illegal runs made by these supply planes were . . . overlooked.

The young guy's directions brought Eleanor to the back of the hangar. She skirted around the building and found the main doors wide open. A large plane took up most of the space inside, its wings almost reaching wall to wall. It was definitely an older model, one that ran on gasoline, not one of the newer electric ones. The plane was thick and round, painted in not-quite-matching shades of white, with a wide belly. Eleanor assumed from its girth it was a cargo plane, and it looked like it had been beaten up and not quite given the chance to heal before it got into another fight. A couple of mechanics currently worked on its nose.

A man stood nearby, watching them, one arm across his chest, the other elbow propped on it, hand under his chin. He wore a plaid shirt under a heavy canvas jacket and had long brown hair that almost reached his collar, a mustache, and thick stubble over the rest of his face and neck.

Eleanor approached him. "Are you Luke?"

He glanced at her, then turned his attention back to the plane. "What do you want?"

"I hear you sometimes fly to the Arctic."

"Who told you that?"

"Just some guys who're jealous of your fat contracts."

"That so? Well, pilots always talk big on the ground, but I don't seem to have a lot of competition these days."

"Are you going up there soon? To the Arctic?"

He scowled. "If these clowns know what they're doing."

"Well, I was wondering if—"

"Ed!" Luke stepped toward the plane. "What are you doing? Radar's working fine—leave it alone!"

Eleanor waited while Ed defended himself and Luke got even angrier. After he'd corrected the mechanic again, he glanced back at Eleanor.

"You're still here."

"I am," she said.

"You must want something."

"I . . ." Eleanor didn't know if she should just come out and say what she wanted. But she didn't know what she would say instead, or how to ask. "I'm—I'm trying to get to the Arctic."

"Uh-huh." He didn't seem at all surprised, and she couldn't tell if that was because *nothing* surprised him, or because he simply didn't believe her. "And?"

"And I want to pay you to take me."

"No way."

She scowled. "Why not?"

"Why not?" He turned to fully face her for the first time since she'd walked into the hangar. "Because you're a kid, and I'm not gonna get myself sued over you. And really, if you're running away from home, why the Arctic?"

Eleanor bristled, for several reasons. "Why does everyone assume I'm running away? I'm *not*."

"No? Then what are you doing here?"

"That's none of your business!" It didn't feel right telling Luke anything about her mom. "*Your* business is getting me to the Arctic."

He shook his head. "Girl, you don't know a thing about my business."

True, but she was pretty sure he liked to get paid, no matter what his business was. "I have money," she said.

"Not gonna happen."

"I'll pay you five hundred dollars."

"No way."

"A thousand."

"Nope."

"Fifteen hundred." She couldn't offer much more than that. She only had two thousand.

"You can make that number as high as you want," Luke said. "Won't change a thing."

"You have to take me."

"I don't have to do anything except get this plane fixed and make my delivery on time."

Eleanor wasn't giving up. "Where are you going?"

He rolled his eyes. "Fairbanks."

"I need to get to Barrow."

"Is that right?"

"Yes. Do you ever fly to Barrow?"

"Not that this'll do you a lick of good, but I'm heading to Barrow after my stop in Fairbanks."

"That's perfect."

He laughed, a hollow sound, even though he seemed genuinely amused. "It's far from perfect," he said. "Barrow is no place for a kid. Last place on earth you want to be, and that's saying something."

"How much do you want?" Eleanor asked.

"It's not the money, kid. I'm doing you a favor."

"Please." Eleanor hated that she couldn't keep the begging sound out of her voice. "If you don't help me, I'm going to be in big trouble."

"Oh, I think you already are."

"What do you mean?"

"Airport security was here just before you were. They're looking for a girl with a big Arctic pack on her back." He made a show of looking around the hangar. "I'm going to go out on a limb here and guess that's you?"

This unsteadied Eleanor's resolve with a moment of panic. She swallowed. "Maybe."

Luke spread his hands. "Look, I'm not going to turn you in. Truth is, I don't care what kind of fight you're in with your parents, or what kind of teenage drama you got yourself into, but—"

"You don't know a thing about me." Her voice actually sounded slightly menacing, which she hadn't intended. But Luke was making light of a dangerous and desperate situation, without knowing it.

He glanced at her askance. "Fact is, I take you on my plane, your problems become my problems. Someone could even say I kidnapped you. No thanks."

"Please, I—"

"Sorry, kid." He swept his greasy hair back. "Now, every moment I waste talking to you is a moment I'm not watching these idiots with *Consuelo*—"

"Who's Consuelo?"

His scowl said he thought she was an idiot for asking. "*My plane.* So if you'll excuse me." He turned away from her.

Eleanor seethed. "I'm not just some runaway, you know! You don't understand the situation! This is—"

"Kid, you find someone on this snowball of a planet who *doesn't* have a sob story, and they're either a lunatic or a liar. Now get lost before I change my mind and call security."

Eleanor accepted then that she wouldn't be able to convince him, so she slowly turned toward the hangar exit and walked away.

But that didn't mean she was giving up. That beat-up plane was going to Barrow. When it—or *she*, apparently— took off, Eleanor planned to be on her.

Eleanor found a couple of giant wooden spools stacked outside the hangar, which she hid behind, stealing occasional glances at Luke's plane through a nearby window. *Consuelo*'s back end lay open, and Eleanor decided that her best chance to stow away would be to get inside her cargo hold. But how? She pushed on the window to test whether it was unlocked.

It was.

She left it open a crack to hear what was going on inside, then waited for an opportunity when no one was around.

She checked her Sync to see what time it was. At least the day had started to warm up a bit. Her teeth weren't chattering, and her body didn't shiver as badly. On the other side of the giant spools, the road had grown busier, with more trucks and people moving between the hangars. An hour went by. Then another.

At last the mechanics seemed to be clearing from *Consuelo*, rolling away their tool chests and unplugging their mobile computer terminals.

Now was Eleanor's chance. She slid the window open the rest of the way and readied herself.

"Thanks, Ed!" she heard Luke call from somewhere near the plane's nose.

The mechanics and ground crew had all backed away, but they were still in the hangar. There was a chance one of them might spot Eleanor, but she didn't think she could wait to see if they would leave before the plane took off.

When no one seemed to be looking, she lifted her pack through the window and dropped it on the ground. Then she quickly heaved herself over the sill and landed next to her pack.

A stair truck pulled slowly up to the plane. Luke trotted up it and then ducked through the aircraft's open door. As the stair truck backed away, and Luke closed the door, Eleanor realized he was leaving. She had to move, and she had to move fast.

She grabbed her pack and skulked along the back wall of the hangar, putting the plane between her and most of the crew, readying herself to run toward the open cargo hold. But just then she heard the whine of hydraulics engaging, and the ramp to the cargo hold lifted off the ground. The plane was closing.

Eleanor couldn't wait until the hangar emptied. She broke cover and sprinted toward the ramp, watching it rise, knee-level, then waist-level, then approaching shoulder-height.

As she reached it, she launched her pack inside ahead of her, heard it slide down the ramp into the plane. Then she jumped, high enough to get her shoulders and elbows over the edge of the ramp, and felt it lift her feet off the ground. If she didn't get inside, she'd either have to let go or let the door close on her.

She pushed and strained upward, managed to kick her left leg over the edge, and from there was able to roll over the lip into the plane. The steep angle of the ramp sent her tumbling downward, and she landed hard at the bottom. The ramp closed with a loud and final clang behind her, sounding like one of those prison doors in the movies.

She was in.

The cargo hold was dark, except for two small windows and a few dim yellow lights in wire cages along the walls. It smelled of old machine oil and gasoline. Within a couple of moments, her eyes adjusted to the low light, and shapes emerged from the darkness.

Stacks of crates and containers surrounded by thick nylon webbing filled the space. Eleanor bumped her way deeper into the hold until she found a small space where she could nestle down and hide for the long flight, which usually took her mom seven or eight hours.

The plane's combustion engines woke up, much louder back here than Eleanor had expected. She covered her ears while the aircraft eased forward, and as the plane left the hangar, the light coming in through the two windows brightened.

Eleanor could now see her surroundings better, the crates and boxes and other containers on all sides. They each bore the same stamp.

PROPERTY OF
G.E.T.

Her eyes widened. Luke's cargo belonged to the G.E.T.? That was his big fat contract? That was probably why he was heading to Barrow. A slow dread overcame her as she realized she might have just walked her Sync right into the hands of the people she had tried to keep from taking it. This stowaway plan had just become a lot more complicated.

As they rumbled along the tarmac, Eleanor gripped

the webbing for support. It was actually fairly cold in the cargo bay, and it occurred to her that the plane might not be heated back here. It might not even be *pressurized* back here, now that she really considered it. As that realization unfolded, Eleanor's dread multiplied into fear.

She could freeze or suffocate long before they even reached Barrow.

⟶ CHAPTER ⟵
7

Aᴛᴇʀ ᴛᴀxɪɪɴɢ ғᴏʀ ᴀ sʜᴏʀᴛ ᴅɪsᴛᴀɴᴄᴇ, ᴛʜᴇ ᴘʟᴀɴᴇ ᴄᴀᴍᴇ to a halt. Eleanor wondered why they weren't taking off, and she worried that it might even have something to do with her. Had security stopped the plane? Then the hydraulics engaged with the same whine as before, and a frame of light appeared around the ramp as it descended. Luke was opening the hold.

Eleanor scrambled deeper into the stacks of G.E.T. cargo, but there wasn't enough space for her to completely hide herself. She looked up, made a lightning decision, and climbed up the webbing as if it were a ladder, which wasn't easy. The straps moved and gave under her feet like the rope ladders on her old elementary school playground. But she managed to reach the top and dive over and inside the webbing, onto the stack of cargo. There she nestled down, now safely out of sight.

Just then, voices entered the cargo hold, followed by the sound of heavy boots on the metal ramp. Eleanor held as still as she could, listening.

"I was just about to take off," Luke said. "This delay is—"

"Pardon my intrusion." That sounded like an old man, with a voice that creaked like leather. "But the nature of this shipment is such that I had to make certain. When did you take delivery?"

"Late last night. Loaded it myself."

"It is all accounted for?" the old man asked.

"I told you, it's all in order." Luke sounded even more irritated with this guy than he had with Eleanor.

"This hold is pressurized? Temperature controlled?"

"Of course."

Well, at least Eleanor wouldn't have to worry about suffocation or freezing to death.

"And now that you've seen it," Luke said, "I'll be on my way. There'll be a major polar storm moving in over Barrow in the next twenty-four hours. I need to be unloaded and gone before it hits."

"When do you expect to land?" the old voice asked.

"Depending on how long my stop in Fairbanks takes—"

"Does your business in Fairbanks involve humanitarian aid?"

"What? No."

"Then by order of article six of the International Conservation of Energy Treaty, I authorize you to proceed directly to Barrow."

"Dr. Watkins," Luke said, "I don't need your authorization to do anything."

"Let me rephrase. I *order* you to go straight to Barrow."

Luke's voice turned angry. "Excuse me? Yours ain't the only cargo on this plane. I've got buyers lined up for the rest of this stuff! I gotta make a profit—"

"I have the power, granted by the UN, to override all but humanitarian missions. You run afoul of me, young man, and I'll make sure this . . . plane is grounded for good. Do I make myself clear?"

"Perfectly," Luke said, bringing a different kind of ice into the plane.

"Good. I'll let our Barrow facility know to expect you."

"We done here?" Luke asked.

"You may depart," the old voice said.

The sound of the men's footsteps left the plane, and

a few minutes later, the cargo door lifted and groaned shut. When the engines kicked back up and the plane moved, the tower of cargo beneath Eleanor shifted as if it might collapse. Her hands and feet shot outward instinctively, to steady herself, but the netting kept it all in place.

The plane taxied for only a short time. Then the engines rose to a wail, and the aircraft lurched forward. Everything around Eleanor rattled so hard, she imagined pieces of the plane shaking off on the runway. The escalating g forces rolled her up against the netting and pressed it into her back as the plane finally heaved itself into the sky. Once the aircraft lost contact with the ground, the rattling ceased and things settled down, as if the plane had let out a sigh. It was still noisy but felt more calm and steady. They were in the air.

Eleanor had made it. Officially an Arctic stowaway. She imagined the city of Phoenix growing small and distant behind her, with its refugees and Ice Castles and her school and her home and . . .

She sighed. "Poor Uncle Jack," she said aloud.

Once they'd been airborne for a while, Eleanor climbed down and felt comfortable pulling out one of the flashlights from her pack to get a better look at the cargo around her. She wondered what the G.E.T. might be sending to the Arctic and hoped it would give her some clue about what her mother had been working on in Barrow. She cast the flashlight's narrow spotlight over the crates and containers, the white circle of cold light a moon moving through the hold, landing on uneven surfaces.

Most of the crates were too heavy or large for her to lift, but she managed to pull down one of the smaller ones, labeled TELLURIC SCANNER. It was made of plastic, with a hinged latch on each side of the lid. She popped them and pulled the lid away.

Inside, she found an electronic device wedged in cutaway foam. It reminded her of the bar-code scanner guns that grocery store employees carried around on their hips. But this looked a lot more complicated, with a couple of blank LCD screens, dials, and buttons. Eleanor had no idea what it might be used for. *Telluric?*

She closed the lid to the case and hoisted it back where it came from. The nearby crates bore labels that made about the same amount of sense to her. There were TELLURIC TRANSISTORS and FIELD PERIMETER RODS and TELLURIC CONDUCTION RODS. She pulled out her Sync, looked up *telluric*, and found it was just a word for something related to the earth.

Great. *Earth.*

Given that her mom was a geologist, and the G.E.T. drilled for oil, this wasn't exactly an astounding discovery.

She sighed and switched off her flashlight to save power. Then she looked around for a comfortable place to sit and couldn't find one. On top of that, the unremitting engine noise had already started to feel like a pressure on her ears.

Eight hours.

This was going to be a long flight.

After an hour of doing nothing, Eleanor turned her attention back to the crates. She forced herself to look at each one, just in case there was something interesting. That took up another hour or so but didn't result in anything new or useful.

She pulled out her Sync, intending to reread her mom's texts, but decided that perhaps she should conserve the device's power. She didn't know when she would next have the opportunity to charge it. But that thought caused a new worry. What if the battery died and she had no way to read the messages? The last message in particular, with the numbers, that code . . . She decided to memorize them, just in case. It didn't take too long. *Just like memorizing a couple of phone numbers.* To test herself, she covered up the screen with her hand and recited the series out loud, checking herself along the way. She got them all right.

She was now over two hours into the flight, with a good five or six to go, and she still had nothing to do.

She ended up unpacking all her gear—the mask, the crampons, the coats, all of it—and then practiced putting it on and taking it off, repeatedly, until the actions became quick and smooth. She timed herself and got to the point where she could suit up completely in under a minute. Even though she had no idea whether that meant anything, it made her feel more ready for the Arctic.

Another hour had gone by.

She walked to one of the two windows and peered outside. Everything just looked white. She turned away from the window—what she thought was a sky full of clouds—but then stopped. She returned to the window and looked down.

White. It wasn't just the sky. It was all white.

The ground had disappeared, as if someone had pulled a white sheet tight over a bed. Eleanor blinked.

The ice sheet.

They'd reached the great glacier's border, the edge of life and civilization, then flown right over it without her realizing it. She'd heard so much about the menace of the ice from school and the news, she'd half expected it to have claws and teeth. But from up here, it appeared quiet and still. Tranquil, even. Somehow, that made it more frightening, because that meant the ice could lie.

She watched the endless white for some time—the ice that had taken her mom—but after a while, its image became distorted. She started seeing things down there. Was that a river? A road? A town? In the same way her eyes imagined shapes and shadows in pitch darkness, she saw signs of life on the ice where there couldn't be any, as though her mind simply refused to accept a void.

She forced herself from the window, back to her gear. Her eyes watered and burned from staring too long. She rubbed them and realized they wanted to stay closed, so she made herself a bed with her coats and her sleeping bag and lay down. They weren't quite halfway yet. Maybe she could sleep for some of the flight.

Eleanor awoke to a sudden jolt. It bounced her hard enough to bang her head on the floor. The whole plane rattled and shook.

They'd landed.

She quickly gathered all her gear and shoved it into

her pack. How long had she slept? Four hours? She hadn't realized she was so exhausted. But her level of stress and fear over the last day had been intense.

The plane lumbered along and eventually settled to a stop with a giant sigh. Eleanor decided it would probably be better to stay out of sight at first. She climbed back up the webbing to her previous perch and settled in to wait.

Before long, the door to the cargo hold opened up, and first light, then wind, and finally snow poured in. The cold hit Eleanor's face like an unexpected slap, and she realized instantly that this was Alaska.

"Your stuff is there," she heard Luke say. His voice had a metallic, muffled quality. "Behind all the G.E.T. cargo."

"You're running shipments for the G.E.T.?" It was a woman's voice, also metallic and muffled.

"Don't have much of a choice, according to the law. They even ordered me to skip your delivery, so if anyone asks, this is all for 'humanitarian purposes.' Article something or other from the International Conservation of Energy Treaty."

Eleanor thought back to the earlier conversation she'd overheard. If she understood Luke correctly, they weren't in Barrow yet. He'd stopped in Fairbanks after all. Her cheeks and nose were already starting to hurt from the cold, and each breath stabbed the inside of her chest with an icicle.

"Well, I appreciate you violating a UN treaty," the woman said.

"Anything for you, doll."

Eleanor could hear them getting closer.

"Any trouble, otherwise?" the woman asked.

"Nope. But I have to hustle the rest of this to Barrow before the storm hits."

"Forecast is saying it's going to be a bruiser." She paused. "What's that?"

"What?"

"That pack."

Oh no. Eleanor closed her eyes. Her pack. She had left it on the floor. Luke knew she was here.

He raised his voice. "Come on out, kid!"

"Kid?" the woman asked.

Eleanor sighed, rose to her hands and knees, and peered over the top of her crate tower. She saw now why their voices had sounded odd. They were both wearing masks—full plates of plastic and metal, with dark lenses over the eyes and a breathing apparatus over the mouth—which was what Eleanor wished she was wearing with each moment her skin was exposed to the Alaskan cold blowing into the cargo bay.

"Get over here," Luke said. "Now."

Eleanor scrambled down the webbing, nervousness making her feel especially clumsy. But what could Luke do at this point? It wasn't like he could just leave her there in Fairbanks, and with his deadline, he wouldn't be turning back to Phoenix, either. He'd be mad, for sure, but she would get to Barrow, which was all that mattered.

Luke folded his arms, and with his mask, he looked a bit more threatening than before. "What do you think you're doing, kid?"

She folded her arms, too. "My name isn't *kid*. It's Eleanor."

"I don't care," Luke said. "You shouldn't be here."

"Oh, Luke, go easy on her," the woman said. "It looks like she had a long flight. Eleanor, I'm Betty."

"Nice to meet you." Eleanor turned to Luke. "I didn't mean any harm. Your plane was the only way."

"The only way to what?" Betty asked.

"The only way to get to Barrow."

"Barrow?" Eleanor could imagine the shock on Betty's face behind her mask. "Why on earth would you want to go—"

"It doesn't matter," Luke said. "Betty, your drilling cores are stacked over there. Be careful—they're heavy."

Betty snorted. "Always a gentleman."

"You know me."

A moment passed, and when it became clear Luke didn't intend to help, Betty went to the crates he'd indicated. She lifted one, and with a backward glance that would probably have been a glare, she marched out of the plane.

Eleanor felt a sudden, violent shiver. Back in Phoenix, she thought she knew cold. But this Alaskan cold had moved its assault from her face to the rest of her body, as if determined to make sure she knew it was something else entirely.

"You need a mask," Luke said. "Did you bring one?"

Eleanor nodded.

"Well, don't just stand there like a fool. Go get it."

Eleanor hurried to her pack, pulled out the mask, and put it on, just as she'd practiced. Her face warmed a little, which felt better, but the biggest difference was the air. It no longer bit on its way into her lungs.

"Better?" Luke asked.

"Better." Her voice had taken on that same metallic muffle.

"Good," he said. "Now get off my plane. This is as far as you go."

"What?" Eleanor almost laughed. He couldn't be serious.

"You heard me." He firmed up his stance. "End of the line. Off. Now."

CHAPTER

8

"LUCIUS FOURNIER!" BETTY HAD COME BACK INTO THE cargo hold. "You are *not* leaving her stranded here."

Lucius?

"Better here than stranded in Barrow," he said.

"I won't be stranded," Eleanor said. "My *mom* is there."

Luke stared at her a moment through the dark lenses of his mask. "Your mom is in Barrow?"

Eleanor hesitated before answering. "Close to Barrow, yes. That's what I've been trying—"

"Why the devil is your mom in Barrow?"

"She's a geologist," Eleanor said. "She works for an oil company."

Luke turned toward Betty.

The woman put her hands on her hips and cocked her head. "Don't look at me that way. You've only got one choice here, and you know it."

Another moment passed, and then Luke flipped both hands in the air. "Fine. Betty, get your crap off my plane. Kid, let's go." He stalked away through the hold.

Eleanor turned to Betty. "Do you need help?"

Betty laughed. "Not as much as you will once this plane takes off. But don't let him fool you. Luke is a good guy underneath all that, and that's a rare thing up here. You better get going, though, unless you want to stay back here for the rest of the flight."

"Thanks." Eleanor grabbed up her pack and followed after Luke. She found him waiting at the bottom of the ramp.

"That all you brought?" he asked.

Eleanor nodded. Then she looked around. She was now immersed in the sea of ice she'd seen from the plane, the sheet flat and unending to the horizon on all sides. They were on an airfield, but the buildings and hangars looked more like battered bunkers. Every vehicle Eleanor saw had tank treads instead of wheels. Every person she saw moving around wore layers and layers of armor against the cold and walked with head and shoulders down. Their appearance created the impression that Fairbanks was a city at war, under constant siege from the cold and the ice.

"This way." Luke led her to the front of the plane, then up a motorized staircase.

Eleanor followed him up and through the door into the cabin.

There were three rows of passenger seats, four to a row, two on each side of the aisle. Luke pulled the door closed, latched it with a big lever, and removed his mask. Then he ducked into the open cockpit at the front and took the pilot's seat.

"Sit anywhere you want," he called over his shoulder as he stretched a headset over his ears.

"Okay." Eleanor took off her mask, replaced it in her pack, and tossed the pack into one of the seats. Then she climbed up into the cockpit and slipped into the copilot's chair beside Luke.

He lifted an eyebrow at her. "What are you doing?"

She buckled in. "You told me to sit anywhere I want."

"Yeah." He jabbed a thumb over his shoulder. "Back there."

90

"That's not what you said."

"Well, I—" He closed his mouth. "You know what? Fine. Whatever. Just don't touch anything."

Eleanor brought her legs up and crossed them in her seat. "I won't."

Luke positioned the headset's microphone in front of his mouth. "Fairbanks Tower, this is cargo craft one-nine-three-zero *Consuelo*, reporting all systems go. . . . Roger that. . . ." He flipped a series of switches around and above him. Eleanor scanned the cockpit, with all its dials and gauges and controls, and noticed a little black-and-white screen with a fish-eyed video feed from the cargo hold. It appeared that Betty had unloaded all her crates. Luke watched the feed carefully for a moment and then flipped another switch. On the screen, the cargo door closed.

Then it occurred to Eleanor. Luke had known she was back there. Had he been watching her *the whole time*? She swiveled in her chair and looked directly at him while pointing at the screen.

He shrugged. "I didn't notice you until we were three hours out of Phoenix, but by that point I'd already lost too much time—" He snapped forward as if listening to something in his headphones. "Affirmative, Fairbanks Tower. Cargo craft one-nine-three-zero *Consuelo*, taxiing to runway." He took hold of the yoke

91

and the throttle, and the plane crawled forward.

Eleanor hadn't taken her stare from him.

As he guided the plane, he shook his head at her. "Don't look at me like that. You're the one who illegally stowed away on my plane."

Eleanor faced forward in her seat. "That doesn't give you the right to spy on me."

"According to ancient maritime law, stowaways have no rights. They can even be thrown overboard."

Eleanor squinted at him. "You just made that up, didn't you?"

"I'm sure I heard it somewhere," he said. The plane reached a position at the end of a long, unpaved runway that appeared to be made of ice mixed with gravel. "Fairbanks Tower, cargo craft one-nine-three-zero *Consuelo*, am I cleared for takeoff? Over."

Eleanor wasn't quite ready to let his lie go, but Luke's focus had shifted entirely to the plane. He took hold of the yoke in front of him.

"Affirmative. See you next time, Fairbanks Tower." He pushed the throttle down again, but this time, the plane jumped, gaining speed fast enough to squeeze Eleanor's stomach. "Here we go, kid," Luke said.

Taking off was a very different experience up here than it had been back in the cargo hold. Through the windows, Eleanor could see ahead of them and to either side, and she felt a thrill at the way the world streaked by.

Luke pulled back on the yoke, and the nose of the plane lifted off the ground, followed by the rest of her, and they were airborne. The plane climbed at a steep angle, the world falling away from them at a rapid pace, and she kept climbing until they were above the clouds.

Several moments later, Luke leveled them off. "About two hours to Barrow."

Eleanor's earlier irritation and embarrassment had faded. Luke might have been spying on her, but that also meant he hadn't kicked her off. "Thanks," she said.

Luke took a moment to respond. "You're welcome."

"So, where are you from?" Eleanor asked.

Luke shook his head. "No. We're not doing that."

"Doing what?"

"Getting to know each other."

Eleanor rolled her eyes and turned to look out the window. "Just trying to pass the time."

The engine droned.

"Anchorage," Luke said. "That's where I'm from."

Maybe that answered the other question Eleanor wanted to ask, which was why Luke kept flying up here when other pilots didn't. "Ever been married? Kids?"

Luke gripped the steering column. "Married once. Two kids. Robbie and Amanda. When the ice came, my ex took them south. I took to the air." He turned to look at Eleanor. "What about you? Your mom's in Barrow. Where's your dad?"

"No dad," she said. "I have an Uncle Jack, though."

"He know where you are?" Luke asked.

An instant guilt put Eleanor on the defensive. Uncle Jack was probably freaking out by now, calling the cops and everything. "I'm sure he has some idea. He'll forgive me, though. Eventually. He gets me."

"That a problem you have? People not getting you?"

"Pretty much," Eleanor said. "People think I'm a freak. Maybe I am. No one I know would have stowed away on a plane heading to Alaska."

"Well," Luke said, "not many pilots are crazy enough to fly up this way, so I guess that makes me a freak, too." He paused. "What about your mom? Does she get you?"

"Sometimes," Eleanor said. But there were also times it didn't seem like her mom, or even Uncle Jack, truly understood her. At times it seemed like no one did. She shook that thought away and focused on the clouds, the blue sky, the blur of ice below. This was much better than riding in the cargo hold.

"So." She bounced an eyebrow. "Lucius, huh?"

He chuckled. "Only when I'm in trouble."

Eleanor grinned. "Betty was right, you know."

"About what?"

"You *are* a good guy."

His demeanor changed. The smile abandoned his lips and his eyes, leaving a hardness behind. "Don't get your hopes up, kid."

For the next hour or so, they didn't say much. The ice sheet below gave way to the peaks of a mountain range pushing up through it, creating the appearance of an island chain. Eleanor started thinking about what she would do when she reached Barrow. The first thing she *wanted* to do was find someone with a snow vehicle she could hire, travel to her mother's station out on the ice sheet, and start helping in the search.

But that might have to wait. It was nearing four o'clock in the afternoon, which meant there wouldn't be a lot of time before the sun set, and even Eleanor knew better than to go out onto the ice sheet at night.

The eastern horizon had grown dark. It took Eleanor a moment to realize it was too early for that to be from the time of day.

"Why is it so dark over there?" she asked Luke.

"Polar storm," he said. "It'll hit Barrow earlier than I was expecting. I'm barely going to have enough time to unload and refuel."

"What happens if you run out of time?" Eleanor asked, but what she worried about more was her mom, stranded or lost or trapped somewhere out there, about to get caught in the same storm. Unless Eleanor managed to locate her first.

"I'm stuck in Barrow until it passes over," Luke said. "Could last a week, or longer." He shook his head. "We'll be landing soon. How quick can your mom come get you?"

Eleanor shifted in her seat. "Um, not quick."

Luke paused. "Why not?"

Eleanor didn't think there was any reason to keep the truth from him now. They were almost at Barrow. "My mom is kind of . . . lost."

"What?"

"She went out on the ice sheet and her company lost contact with her."

"Okay, so who's coming to get you?"

Eleanor's voice got quiet. "No one."

Luke's face reddened. "Is anyone up here even expecting you?"

"No," she said.

"Ice me, I knew something was off," Luke said. "Should have listened to my gut and kicked you off back in Fairbanks. After I unload and refuel, I'm taking you back to Phoenix—"

"NO!"

"You don't have a choice, kid."

"I'm not leaving until I find my mom. I'm the only one she trusted, and I'm going after her!"

"Well, I don't know any mom who would want her kid daughter coming up to Barrow, of all places, all alone on some rescue mission."

"I didn't say she wanted me to come," Eleanor said. "I *chose* to come up and find her." She sat back in her seat, arms folded. "It doesn't matter—it's not your problem. After we land, you don't have to worry about me anymore."

Luke closed his eyes and kneaded his forehead. His voice got quiet. "Listen to me very carefully. Barrow is a dangerous place, even for people like me. Especially for someone like you. It's like the Wild West up here, kid. Excepting a few scientists like your mom, most of the people up here are criminals running from the law, or desperate folks trying to strike it rich. Lots of people get stuck up here in forced labor outfits. Drill junkies murder each other over oil claims. You don't have any idea what you're doing."

Eleanor knew all that, but thinking about it only made her frightened, and she didn't want to be frightened. She wanted to find her mom. But Luke seemed genuinely concerned for her. For the first time since leaving Phoenix, she began to really doubt her plan.

"When we land," Luke said, "just stay on the plane. Okay? I'll have you back home, safe and sound, by early tomorrow morning."

Eleanor didn't respond. She didn't know what to say. She stared out the window, watching the darkness on the horizon deepen and spread, taking over the sky.

Luke didn't say anything for the rest of the flight either, until a short while later, when he radioed the Barrow Tower, asking for permission to land.

Eleanor spotted the first drilling rig down on the ice, a black spider against that white sheet. Then she spotted another, and another. A whole network of drilling facilities and a web of interconnecting pipelines between them, all leading to the city of Barrow at the center.

"Buckle in," Luke told Eleanor. "With that storm coming, it's going to be a bumpy descent."

The turbulence buffeted and jolted them on the way down, hard enough that Eleanor was glad for her seat belt. Her stomach lurched and groaned, and she spent most of the ride down holding on to the sides of the pilot's chair, eyes fixed on the bouncing, narrow runway and the scattering of buildings now coming into view.

When they finally touched down, hard, she let out a sigh that deflated her whole body. Luke did some more talking with the flight tower, and as they taxied toward a large hangar, Eleanor thought about what she was going to do now.

She'd come this far. She had her Sync, with the information her mom had sent, and she had her gear. Her mom had friends up here at the research station, too, the other scientists and workers from her oil company. She was sure they had to come into Barrow pretty frequently. Perhaps if Eleanor could make contact with them, they'd come get her, and then they could all find her mom together.

She noticed Luke watching her from the corner of his eye.

"What?" she asked.

"You're staying on the plane, right?"

"Right."

He raised an eyebrow.

"Yes, I am," she said. He'd forgive her lie quickly enough when he didn't have some kid to worry about anymore.

"Okay, then," he said.

They reached the hangar, which resembled a military bunker in the same way the buildings had in Fairbanks. Luke pulled the plane up alongside its enormous, heavy doors, which slowly opened at their approach. Workers filed out wearing full polar gear, their coats emblazoned with the G.E.T. logo. Their presence worried Eleanor, even though she didn't think they could possibly know who she was.

"Good," Luke said. "They're ready for me. We might just beat the storm."

He killed the plane's engines and hit the switch for the cargo bay door. Eleanor watched it open in the video monitor. Luke got out of his seat and left the cockpit.

"I'll say it one more time: You just sit tight in here." He put on his mask, gloves, and coat. "Got it?"

"Got it," Eleanor said.

He pulled the latch to open the door, and the Arctic cold forced its way into the plane. Eleanor shivered but waited in her seat. After he'd left, she watched the monitor, the G.E.T. crew marching into the cargo bay, undoing the straps, taking down the towers of crates. Soon Luke was there, directing them. Eleanor waited until he appeared completely involved in the unloading, and then she left the cockpit.

In the main cabin, she pulled on her own gear. Mask, gloves, coats, all of it. She slung her pack up on her back, and with one last glance at the monitor to make sure Luke was still distracted, she opened the door.

Outside, the air and the cold seemed even harsher somehow than they had in Fairbanks. Perhaps it was the towering wall of darkness approaching from the east. Perhaps it was the low light of the late-afternoon sun, skirting the horizon. But Eleanor was glad for all her gear, and for now, she felt protected and safe. She just had to get to town and then somehow get to her mom's station before the storm hit.

She descended the mobile stairway and reached the frozen tarmac. G.E.T. crew scrambled nearby, but no one paid her any mind at all. She looked around, and a short distance off, she spotted the cluster of buildings she'd seen from the air. They seemed to huddle together, forlorn and insignificant against the immensity of the icy horizon, an isolated outpost that shouldn't even be here.

Barrow.

With one last glance at the *Consuelo*, she set off toward it.

— CHAPTER —
9

THE CITY OF BARROW WASN'T A CITY—AT LEAST NOT LIKE any city Eleanor knew. Instead, it was a collection of fortresses, each building apparently constructed with nothing in mind but defense. No paint, no decoration of any kind. Just masses of wood, concrete, and steel. Most of them were shaped like domes, some of them like fat cylinders, others like Quonset huts. They all seemed to have air locks, too, with tunnels between their outer and inner doors.

All the people Eleanor saw moved among these buildings with the same forward-leaning trudge, like trees that had grown up in a permanent wind. It felt like several of them were staring at her as she walked through town, though because of their face masks, she couldn't be sure.

Eleanor didn't know exactly what she was looking for. She needed to talk to someone who might know how she could contact her mom's facility. The best place for that would probably be some kind of gathering spot. A store. A post office. A restaurant. Did they have any of that up here?

She hadn't yet seen any obvious signs on the buildings. A few had stenciled numbers and letters that might be helpful if Eleanor knew what they meant. But she did spot a building with a row of snowmobiles parked out front. They reminded her of the trucks parked outside the Prop Stop Cafe, so she decided to try there first.

When she reached it, she saw that this building did have a sign: a carved wooden one with a palm tree, a hula dancer, and the word CANTINA, little flecks of chipped paint hanging on in the deepest cracks, the rest having been ice-blasted away.

As she reached for the door, it opened. A large man ducked out, then unbent to his full height. He wore a mask like her, but in addition to his coats, he wore the dingy white pelt of a polar bear, an animal that had long since vanished from the Arctic. Eleanor could smell the sharp, unwashed musk of the fur, and maybe the man, through her mask.

He noticed her and stopped. He said nothing, just stared down at her. Beneath his blank gaze, unease crawled up Eleanor's back. She nodded toward him and moved for the door. As she opened it and stepped through, she felt him turn behind her to follow her inside the air lock, so she hurried to the inner door on the opposite end.

But inside the Cantina, Eleanor's unease only grew as every man and woman turned to stare at her. Indoors, she saw the faces beneath the Arctic masks, and they were all as weather-scoured as the buildings. Skin that looked burned. Ragged noses missing their tips, hands missing fingers, the carnage of frostbite. Red, sun-damaged eyes. Some of the men grinned at Eleanor, but in a way that made her want to run, and the smell of the place, unwashed bodies and alcohol, kept getting worse.

She kept her mask on. She'd picked the wrong building. The *very* wrong building.

Eleanor was about to turn and leave, but the big guy from outside had come in behind her and now blocked the door.

"Something I can do for you . . . miss?" the bartender asked. He leaned toward her, arms out straight against the bar like struts, and his tone suggested he couldn't tell whether Eleanor was a boy or a girl under her polar gear.

Her voice was about to give it away. "Um, I'm trying to reach my mom's oil company."

"Which company would that be?" a man asked from a nearby table.

"Sohn International," Eleanor said.

"Don't see those folks too often," the bartender said. "Least, not in here."

Several of the men and women laughed at that. But it was an ugly sound. The stuff Luke had said about the people up here replayed in Eleanor's mind. She started to tremble.

"Do you—do you know how I could reach them?" she asked.

"Try the claims office," the bartender said. "They, uh—they manage all the drilling rights."

Another laugh.

"Thanks," Eleanor said. "Do you— Where is the claims office?"

"I'll show you," said the man standing behind her. He still hadn't removed his mask.

"I . . ." Eleanor was *not* comfortable with that.

"It ain't far, miss," the bartender said. "Boar here can take you there."

Boar? The giant nodded and left through the door.

Eleanor didn't want to go with him, but she really didn't want to stay in here, either. The smell and the stares were becoming unbearable. She decided to just let this Boar man point her in the right direction, and nothing more. She thanked the bartender again and exited the Cantina.

Boar stood outside, waiting. "Ready?"

"I don't want to trouble you," Eleanor said. "You can just give me directions."

He shook his head. "Better if I show you. It's about to get pretty nasty."

He was talking about the storm, which seemed to have doubled the speed of its charge. A heavy wind had picked up, and Eleanor felt herself canting against it. Half the sky roiled with the storm's ferocity, and the setting sun had long since been obscured by its advance. She hoped Luke had managed to take off. And she hoped wherever her mom was, she had shelter.

"Coming?" Boar asked, but didn't wait for her answer before stalking away.

She thought about going the other way and looking for the office on her own, but the storm frightened her, and she didn't want to get caught outside in it. She decided to follow Boar and just maintain a comfortable distance from him.

They passed several more buildings, but with the

storm and nightfall both approaching, there weren't as many people out in the streets. The ones who were seemed wary of Boar but showed the same disconcerting interest in Eleanor.

They turned down a few more streets, and the buildings shrank in size and number. Eleanor didn't know her way around Barrow, but it seemed like they were walking to the edge of town, not toward the center where she would expect a government claims office to be.

"Where is it from here?" she called to Boar, raising her voice over the growing howl of the wind.

He stopped and waited until she'd caught up to him. "What?"

"Where is it?"

"Just up there." He gestured down the road.

Eleanor looked, and all she saw were three more buildings that appeared abandoned, and beyond that, the open expanse of the ice sheet. Then she noticed the snowmobile waiting there, and a sudden fear screamed in her mind louder than the wind. She didn't know where this man planned to take her, or what he planned to do with her, but she had to get away. *Now.*

"Th-thanks, but I just remembered my mom—"

"Don't."

"Don't?"

Boar lunged for her, so fast she couldn't react in time, and grabbed her up, pack and all, under one of his arms. She screamed and kicked and pummeled him, but with all their polar gear, it felt like punching a pillow. He carried her toward the snowmobile, squeezing her so tight her pack dug into her back, and she couldn't catch enough breath to scream. But she tried.

"HELP!" The wind seemed to swallow up what little she got out. "HELP ME!"

They were only a few feet from the snowmobile. She thrashed, as wildly as she could, snarling inside her face mask.

"Cut it out," Boar said. "I just want your gear—"

Something slammed into them, hard, sending them both sprawling on the ground. Freed from Boar's grasp, Eleanor scrambled away from him and shot to her feet. Boar did the same, facing someone new.

Luke.

Eleanor felt an overwhelming gratitude and relief at the sight of him. He stood tall, pointing a pistol at Boar. "Stealing from a kid?" he said. There was a menace in his voice Eleanor hadn't heard before. "Just get on your rig and ride."

Boar's broad shoulders heaved up and down, as if he were breathing hard through his mask. Even with a gun pointed at him, he didn't budge.

"Come here, kid," Luke said. With his free hand, he gestured for Eleanor.

She rushed over to him, and he extended his arm around her, shepherding her behind him.

"Gimme the pack," Boar said. "It's mine."

Luke took an aggressive step toward him. "You get on your rig and ride. Now. Or I'll do you right here."

Boar still didn't move.

"NOW!" Luke fired a shot in the snow at the giant's feet, kicking up a plume of white that the wind then instantly shredded.

Boar flinched, barely, and moved toward his snowmobile. He climbed on, unhurried, and said, "This ain't over," before starting the vehicle's high-pitched engine. A second later, he cranked the handle, and the snowmobile leaped forward, chewing up the snow as it sped out of town.

Luke watched him go for several moments, probably making sure he wasn't going to turn back, the cloud of white in Boar's wake growing smaller and smaller.

Eleanor threw her arms around Luke. "Thank you. Thank you."

He didn't hug her back. "What the hell were you thinking?"

She let go of him and pulled away. "I'm going to find my mom."

"No," he said. "What you're doing is getting yourself robbed. Or worse."

Eleanor didn't want to think about that. "Luke, I—"

"LISTEN!" The fury in his voice came pouring through his mask. "You're damn lucky all he wanted was your gear! Do you know what could have happened to you?"

She did. And when he forced her to examine it, she felt like throwing up. Tears of fear and relief filled her eyes, and her voice fell to a whisper. "I know, I just—"

"Just NOTHING! There is no just anything!" It sounded like some of the anger had left his voice, and now she heard *his* fear. "This is exactly what I warned you about!"

"I know!" Eleanor said. She couldn't keep the choke of tears from her voice.

Luke fell silent. The storm had only intensified around them, shrinking the range of visibility, and even with the protection of all her polar gear, Eleanor could feel some of the cold breaking through.

"From this moment forward," Luke said, "you will do exactly what I say, or so help me, I will tie you up in my cargo bay. Do you understand me?"

She knew that meant she would be flying out on his plane. Back to Phoenix, without her mom. But the experience with Boar had shaken her badly enough that she couldn't fight him. "Yes," she said. "I understand."

"Do you?"

"Yes!"

He nodded. "Okay then." He turned and walked back toward the middle of town.

Eleanor followed him. "Where are we going?"

"Not my plane, if that's what you're asking." He looked around, at the snow the polar storm had already begun to throw at them. "It's too late to take off. I'm not flying anywhere in this."

Eleanor felt like that was her fault. "I'm sorry."

"The storm ain't your doing," Luke said. "But you should be grateful for it. Otherwise, I'd have been long gone, and you'd be . . ."

He didn't finish that statement, and Eleanor didn't want him to.

"We're going to a . . . friend of mine," Luke said. "Betty wouldn't call him a good guy, but he's better than most around here."

The streets were completely deserted now. The wind tore through with its continuous onslaught of snow and ice. It felt like the temperature had simply collapsed, plunging Eleanor into a cold that her mask couldn't keep at bay. She felt it deep in her lungs. Her fingers and toes numbed. This was a polar storm, and she had no doubts that it wanted to kill her.

She could see only a few yards in any direction. The white erased the rest. But the white was fading to gray, and soon it would be night.

They passed several stubborn buildings, which did their job as bulwarks for those inside, until they arrived at one of the larger Quonset huts Eleanor had seen. Luke led the way to the outer door, opened it, and entered the air lock. Eleanor followed him in and forced the door shut behind her.

Though the storm persisted on the other side, they had escaped it. "I'm glad the door wasn't locked."

"Outer doors have to stay unlocked at all times," Luke said. "Arctic Code."

"Arctic Code?" Eleanor asked.

"Unwritten laws. You can secure your inner doors, but you have to keep the air locks open. Gives people a place to escape a storm in an emergency."

"Oh."

"Let's see if Felipe is home." Luke walked to the inner door and pounded on it. They heard someone moving on the other side and, a moment later, the turning of a lock. The door opened.

A brick of a man stood in the doorway, wearing a thick, corded sweater of charcoal gray with suede shoulder pads. His bronze skin bore deep crevices.

"Well, look at this," he said. "A couple of idiots caught in the storm."

Luke took off his face mask. "I'm smart enough not to live in this godforsaken place. How you doing, Felipe?"

Felipe smiled. "Good, Luke, good. Who's this?"

Eleanor became conscious of her own face mask and took it off.

"This is Eleanor," Luke said. "Her mom's a geologist with one of the oil outfits."

Felipe nodded and smiled. Eleanor smiled back.

"You going to let us in?" Luke said. "Or do we have to wait out the storm in your air lock?"

Felipe opened his door wide. *"Bienvenidos."*

Eleanor followed Luke through the door, and they entered a large space filled with snowmobiles and other vehicles, most of them partly disassembled. Machine parts, tools, and lots of equipment Eleanor didn't recognize covered the ground and the walls, and the air inside smelled greased. It seemed Felipe was a mechanic.

"Looks like business is good," Luke said.

Felipe chortled. "I wish. Most of these have been sitting here for months. Their owners can't pay, and until they do, I'm not putting them back together. Back home, I would have already sold them to get them out

113

of my shop, but up here, there's no one to buy them."

"Sorry to hear that," Luke said.

"Could be worse." Felipe shrugged and smiled. "I could be dead."

Eleanor grinned at that.

"We need a place to spend the night," Luke said.

"*Consuelo?*" Felipe asked.

"G.E.T. pulled her out of the storm into their hangar. She's locked up tight until tomorrow."

"I see." Felipe turned to Eleanor. "I named his plane, you know. After my sister. She lives in Phoenix."

"That's where I live," Eleanor said, and as the words came out, she felt a surprising wave of homesickness break over her.

"I like Phoenix," Felipe said. "Sometimes, I wish I could live there. But my sister would probably turn me in."

Turn him in for what? Eleanor resisted the temptation to ask.

"Please," Felipe said. "Take off your gear. Make yourselves comfortable."

"Thank you," Luke said.

Felipe led them to a corner of the shop he had partitioned with makeshift walls, creating the space where it seemed he lived. He had a cot, a small refrigerator, a cookstove, and underneath it all, a dingy woven rug.

Something simmered on the stove. It smelled like chili.

"It's canned," Felipe said. "But you're welcome to have some."

With the smell and offer of food, Eleanor realized that she was starving. She ate her bowl quickly, and the chili's heat, both from the spices and the stove, warmed her through. After they'd finished eating, and Felipe had washed the bowls, they settled in. Felipe rounded up a few extra blankets for Luke, and as Eleanor unrolled her sleeping bag, Luke nudged her over, placing his blankets between her and Felipe's cot.

A short while later, everyone in bed, Eleanor lay awake in the darkness, listening to the storm tearing at the Quonset hut outside. The earlier homesickness lingered, and right now, more than anything, she wished she could be in her own room, in her own warm bed. Uncle Jack would be on the couch downstairs. Her mom would . . . It hit Eleanor then that even if she were back in Phoenix right now, her mom wouldn't be. She'd still be lost on the ice, in this very storm, at the top of the world.

"You awake, kid?" Luke whispered in the darkness beside her.

"Yes."

Felipe let out a snore from his cot.

"Luke?"

"Yeah?"

"What would Felipe's sister turn him in for?"

He was silent.

"Luke?"

"The world's become a crazy place, kid. People do all kinds of things to get by. To survive. Not all those things are legal. Hard to say whose fault that is, really."

Eleanor had certainly broken her share of laws that day. When she looked at everything she'd done from the outside—how Jenna or Claire might see it—she almost couldn't believe she was here, sleeping on the floor of a snowmobile mechanic's shop in Barrow, Alaska. She really was a freak. And yet, she felt entirely justified in every choice she'd made.

But it hadn't been enough. Barrow had defeated her almost as soon as she'd arrived. If Luke hadn't come, it might have robbed her or worse. Eleanor had hoped to somehow get to her mom quickly, before the storm, but realized now how stupid that hope had been. What could she accomplish in the face of such hostility, both from the Arctic and its inhabitants? Who did she think she was? She had failed.

That thought, and the howling wind, followed her into sleep.

─ CHAPTER ─
10

ELEANOR AWOKE TO THE SMELL OF BACON AND EGGS FRY-ing. Felipe stood at the stove, working the spatula, while Luke sat nearby, pulling on his boots. The storm outside didn't sound like it was even thinking about giving up. Eleanor sat upright, rubbed her eyes, and stretched. Her sleep had been heavy, and it took a few groggy moments of blinking to haul her mind to full alertness.

"I'm telling you," Felipe said, "something is going on."

"It's the G.E.T.," Luke said. "Something is always going on."

Felipe shook his head and grabbed a plate. "This

117

is different." He served up a scoop of scrambled eggs, laid on a couple of slices of bacon, and passed the plate to Luke. "A few weeks ago, they cleaned house, fired all the contract drillers. It's all salary men from down south now. People up here are hurting."

Eleanor wondered if that had anything to do with the reason her mom had begun working with the G.E.T., that oil deposit Uncle Jack had mentioned.

"Maybe they're just trying to make their operations legitimate." Luke took a bite of his eggs. "It's about time."

"Maybe." Felipe dished up another plate the same way and brought it to Eleanor.

"Thanks," she said.

Felipe nodded. "But there's more. Guys are seeing stuff out on the ice. Hard guys who've seen everything. And they're spooked, man."

"What are they seeing?" Luke asked.

Felipe sat down on his cot. "Wolves. A pack of wolves, man."

At that, the last veil of Eleanor's tiredness fell away.

Luke stopped chewing. "That's impossible. A pack of wolves can't survive out there."

Eleanor agreed with him. *Nothing* could survive out there. A lot of Arctic species had gone extinct soon after the Freeze set in, and the rest had slowly migrated south. There were now polar bears swimming in the Great Lakes.

"I'm telling you," Felipe said, "they're seeing wolves. Not only that, but they say that sometimes, they see the wolves pulling a hunter on a sled."

"Come on—" Luke laughed and almost choked on his food. "They're just messing with you."

"Not these guys." Felipe shook his head. "One of them won't even go out there anymore. He hasn't worked the drills in weeks."

"What do you think they're seeing?" Eleanor asked.

"I think it's ghosts," Felipe said.

"Ghosts." Luke put his plate down. "You're serious? Ghosts?"

Felipe sat up straight and gave an emphatic nod. "Yes. The ghost of an Inupiat hunter, maybe. And this one guy said he saw something else."

The Inupiat had been an Arctic people, before the ice had driven them south like everyone else. Eleanor leaned closer. She hadn't taken a single bite of her food. "What else did he see?"

"He didn't know," Felipe said. "He was in a storm. Not as bad as this one, but he couldn't see well. He just said it was big. Something very big. He was too scared to get close to it."

"Bigfoot," Luke said. "Gotta be Bigfoot."

Felipe scowled. "You're a pilot. You land, spend a couple of days in town, and then you take off. What do you know about the Arctic?"

"I know what minus a hundred degrees Celsius means," Luke said. "It means the only things living out there are bacteria and viruses."

Eleanor knew Luke was right. Her mom's scientist voice had managed to become a part of her thoughts over the years. But she wanted to believe Felipe's stories, too. She looked down at her plate, remembered her food, and took a bite of bacon.

"You like it?" Felipe asked her.

"Who doesn't like bacon?" Eleanor said.

"True, true." He turned to Luke. "Why is she with you, anyway?"

Luke shrugged. "Ask her. I'm *still* trying to figure that out."

Felipe looked at her.

Eleanor finished chewing and swallowed. "My mom works for one of the oil companies up here. She's missing. I came up to find her."

"That's your mother? *That* geologist?"

"Yeah," Eleanor said. "Wait—you've heard about her?"

"It's all over town. The G.E.T. has been recruiting volunteers for the search."

That gave Eleanor hope. She stood up, her sleeping bag sliding down to her feet. "Have they found anything?"

Felipe scratched his head. "I'm sorry. Not that I've heard."

Eleanor dismissed any discouragement that might have caused, because what he'd said had given her an idea. "Where do they recruit the volunteers?"

"At the claims office," Felipe said. "But they won't be searching in this storm."

It still seemed worth a try to check it out, especially since Eleanor had wanted to go there yesterday. She turned to Luke. "I'm going."

Luke put his hands behind his head, arched his back over his chair, and looked up at the ceiling. He held that position for a moment and then released it with an exasperated sigh. "Fine," he said. "I'll go with you. We're grounded, anyway."

Eleanor hurried into her gear while Luke did the same more slowly. Felipe switched on some classical music and went to work on the engine of a snowmobile. As they were about to leave, he called to Luke, then met them at the door with a rag in his hand.

"You need?" He unwrapped the rag, revealing a small revolver.

Luke gave his chest a pat. "Got it covered."

Felipe nodded and opened the door for them. Eleanor walked through, but the casual routineness of that moment disturbed her, a reminder of where they were and what had happened the day before. She paused in the air lock, grateful for Luke at her side.

Luke put his mask on. "You all right?"

"Thank you," she said.

"Don't thank me yet."

"No, really. Thank you."

Luke rolled his eyes. "C'mon, kid, don't get all mushy. Let's just do this, okay? Put your mask on."

Eleanor did what he asked and then slung her pack over her shoulders. Luke opened the outer door, and the storm invaded the air lock as if it had been waiting for the opportunity. Luke led the way outside, and Eleanor pushed after him, closing the air lock behind her.

The town looked the same as it had the previous day, except for the additional two feet of snow that had piled up in the streets, with storm-blown banks even higher than that against the buildings. With the wind trying to take her down, and the snow up to her knees, the walk to the claims office was arduous.

"Walk in my footsteps!" Luke called over the wind.

He plowed ahead, opening up the snow with his bigger boots, making the trek a bit easier for her. They passed several streets and dozens of buildings without seeing anyone else. But they crossed a few trails of fading footprints, which the storm now worked hard to scrub out.

Before long, they reached the claims office. Luke opened the door and waited until Eleanor was through before he entered and shut it behind them.

Eleanor stamped the snow off her legs and boots, then removed her mask. "We made it."

"Just another day at the North Pole," Luke said, taking off his own mask. He pointed at the inner door. "After you."

Eleanor opened it and stepped into a building that looked like it blended a police station with a doctor's office. Men in camouflage military uniforms stood guard, armed with guns a lot bigger than Luke's pistol, while behind the front counter, through a set of glass sliding doors, a handful of men worked in lab coats at their desks.

The counter had a buzzer, which Eleanor pushed, because the expressionless military guys didn't give the impression of being very amenable to answering her questions. One of the lab-coat guys looked up at the sound of the buzzer, saw Eleanor and Luke, and came to the sliding glass doors. They opened with a whoosh, and he stepped through.

"Can I help you?"

"I'm Eleanor Perry. I'm here about my mom."

The man's forehead wrinkled. "I'm sorry. Who did you say you were?"

"Eleanor Perry. Dr. Perry's daughter."

His eyes widened. "Good Lord! What on earth are you doing here? Why did—? How did you—? I don't—" The words stopped, but his mouth hung open.

"That about sums it up," Luke said.

"I came to help find my mom," Eleanor said. "I heard they recruit the search parties here."

"That's true, they—" The man blinked and shook his head. "Eleanor? That was your name?"

"Yes."

"Does the research station know you're here?"

"No," Eleanor said.

The man nodded. "Let me go radio them. I'm sure they'll want to know. I'll be right back. Okay?"

This was exactly what Eleanor had hoped for. "Okay," she said. She didn't know who she could trust up here, aside from Luke. Her best and only option would be her mother's Sohn International coworkers, people she'd known for years, but Eleanor would have to keep the Sync hidden, even from them.

The man hurried through the sliding doors, leaving Eleanor and Luke alone with the military guys, who didn't appear to have moved.

"Hey," Eleanor said to the nearest one, her mood lifting higher than it had in a couple of days.

He gave her an almost imperceptible nod in reply but said nothing.

Eleanor leaned toward Luke and whispered, "Why are they here? What's a claims office, anyway?"

"This is where they test oil samples and authorize drilling claims," he said. "If a prospector hears something he doesn't like on either score, things can get dangerous."

"Oh."

A few moments later, the sliding doors whooshed open again. "Okay," the lab-coat guy said, "I spoke with the station, and they're sending an armored transport for you."

Eleanor nearly jumped. "Really? When?"

"Right now," the man said. "They should be here in an hour."

This was the best possible outcome. Eleanor would be able to help in the search, perhaps even find a way to use the information her mother had sent, if she could do so without revealing the Sync. And she'd be much safer out at the research station with her mom's coworkers than she was here in Barrow. Then, as soon as the storm lifted, Luke would be able to leave without worrying about her.

They waited there at the office, and a little under an hour later, the lab-coat guy returned to let them know the transport had reached the city perimeter and would be out front shortly.

Eleanor gathered her things and rushed through the door, into the air lock. She'd reached the outer door and was about to open it when Luke called to her.

"Hold on, kid!"

She looked back at him.

He was putting his mask on. "Forgetting something?"

"Oh, right. But the transport is just—"

"*Always* put your mask on. Arctic Code. You promised you'd do whatever I told you, and I'm telling you to do this."

Eleanor groaned but did what he asked. After she had put on her mask, and then her pack, she opened the door and felt instantly glad she'd listened to him as the storm rushed inward, clawing at her face. Eleanor shouldered her way through it and went outside. Luke followed, and a moment later, he pointed down the street, through the blizzard.

"I think I see it."

Eleanor squinted, and then she saw it too. An indistinct shadow, which grew larger and more defined as it came closer. The sound of its engine and the grinding of its tread soon reached her over the roar of the storm, and then, like a whale breaching the ocean surface, the transport lunged fully into view.

It looked to Eleanor like a long, narrow tank, but without the gun, made to withstand this environment in the same way the buildings of Barrow had been. It charged through the snow toward them, and Eleanor waited off to the side until it skidded to a halt before her.

That was when she saw the painted decal, and a sudden panic sent her a step backward.

This was a G.E.T. transport.

Eleanor should have expected this, if she'd stopped to think about it. Her mom had apparently been working with the G.E.T., and they were the ones now searching for her. But she'd naively expected that the transport would be someone from her mom's old company. Not the very people she was trying to avoid. *Stupid, stupid.*

"That's quite a ride," Luke said.

Eleanor stared at the letters. "Yeah."

A hatch on the transport opened, and a G.E.T. crewman leaned out, waving his arm in a rapid pinwheel, motioning Eleanor aboard. She hesitated but quickly realized she had no other option than to climb in. She couldn't stay in Barrow, and now her mom's station knew she was here. She turned to say good-bye to Luke, but he'd taken a step toward the transport, as if he meant to join her.

"Are you coming?" she asked.

"Figured I could help with the search," he said. "Got nothing else to do until the storm passes. Besides, if something happens to you before you find your mom, it's on me."

She smiled behind her mask, happy for his company, and wondered when that had changed. Through the hatch, Eleanor entered a cramped compartment, with a row of seats along both walls, facing one another. She let herself fall into one of the seats, and Luke took the one next to her.

The transport was empty, except for the crewman who had ushered them on and another person sitting opposite them. The crewman closed the hatch and shuffled up through the compartment toward the front of the transport, bumping Luke's and Eleanor's knees as he passed. When he reached the end of the cabin, he opened another hatch to reveal a cockpit with a single driver's seat. He climbed in and closed the hatch behind him.

"Eleanor Perry?" said the other passenger. It was a woman's voice.

"Yes," Eleanor said.

"I'm Dr. Beth Marcus." The woman removed her mask. She was younger than Eleanor's mom, maybe in her late twenties, with slick black hair cut in a sharp jawline bob. "I work with your mom."

Eleanor pulled her own mask off. Her mom had never mentioned a Dr. Marcus before, but finding out things her mom hadn't told her was starting to feel like a common occurrence. Next to Eleanor, Luke pulled his mask off as well.

"I can't tell you how surprised we are to see you here," Dr. Marcus said. "Your uncle has been terribly worried about you."

"You've talked to Uncle Jack?"

"Not personally, no. But we sent some of our people to your house. When they discovered you were gone, your uncle tried telling them you might try to get up here. No one believed him or thought it possible." She shook her head and held out her hands. "But here you are."

"Don't underestimate this one," Luke said, nodding toward Eleanor. "I learned that the hard way."

Dr. Marcus pursed her lips into a tight grin. "And you are?"

"Luke Fournier. Eleanor stowed away on my plane."

"Fournier, yes, you brought in our latest shipment,"

Dr. Marcus said. "Pleasure to meet you." She turned her attention back to Eleanor. "Oh, my dear, we at the Global Energy Trust are so relieved to find you safe and sound. We've already made contact with your uncle to let him know."

"Thank you," Eleanor said. "Can I talk to him?"

"Soon. Once we reach our facility." She shook her head and held out her hands again. "I'm still just so astonished you made it up here."

Eleanor didn't know whether to take that as a compliment or an insult. "My mom would have done the same for me."

"Of that I'm sure," Dr. Marcus said. "She speaks of you constantly, and with great affection."

Something about this woman felt a bit too polished. Like a buffed veneer, all for show. "I just want to find her," Eleanor said.

"As do we all," Dr. Marcus said. "And we're hopeful that you might have access to new information that will help us locate her."

Eleanor was pretty sure Dr. Marcus was talking about her Sync, which was in Eleanor's pack right now, its presence acute, her mother's warning loud in her memory.

Show no one.

Eleanor had left her home to save her mom, but

also to prevent the G.E.T. from taking the Sync. And yet here she was, carrying the device onto a G.E.T. transport.

No one could know she had brought the Sync with her.

— CHAPTER —
11

THE TRANSPORT CHEWED ACROSS THE ICE SHEET, BUT NOT easily. The engines roared as if in competition with the storm, and the uneven surface of the ice jarred and banged Eleanor around in her seat. Through the few portholes lining the compartment, she glimpsed a world outside made blank. An absence of any color, object, or horizon. A nothing world. It felt like they were crossing an ocean, scrambling in their armored boat from one tiny island to another.

Luke had leaned back, feet propped up on the seat opposite him, his eyes closed. Eleanor thought he might have dozed off. Dr. Marcus's earlier effusion at Eleanor's presence had settled into a mild delight, which she displayed through a permanent half smile that Eleanor still thought fake.

"So what was my mom working on?" Eleanor asked.

Dr. Marcus blinked but kept the smile in place. "Oh, just routine analysis. Nothing dangerous or risky, I assure you."

"That's good," Eleanor said, but then she frowned. That answer seemed calibrated to satisfy a question she hadn't asked. Dr. Marcus hadn't answered her real question. Eleanor had grown up around researchers and professors—they weren't exactly known for their people skills. This woman seemed less like a scientist with each mile the transport ground underfoot.

"Doctor of what?" Eleanor asked.

"Pardon me?" Dr. Marcus asked.

"What's your PhD in?"

The perma-smile broke. Just a crack. "Oh." Dr. Marcus waved away the question. "That was ages ago."

Ages ago? No more than ten years, tops. And again, she hadn't answered Eleanor's question. "But what did you study?"

Dr. Marcus cocked her head, her bob falling away from her cheek like a curtain. "International relations," she said.

So she wasn't a scientist. She was in public relations. A diplomat. What was she doing in the Arctic?

"Not much to relate to up here," Luke said, eyes still closed. Apparently, he wasn't asleep. "International or otherwise."

Dr. Marcus folded her gloved hands on her lap. "The G.E.T. has numerous global interests, Mr. Fournier. Foreign nationals and dignitaries visit our facilities regularly. My job takes me from the equator to the North Pole."

Luke opened his eyes. "And which foreign dignitaries are up here right now?"

"I'm afraid that's confidential," Dr. Marcus said.

"Course it is." He closed his eyes again.

No one spoke for the next several miles. Their trek across the ice was taking longer than Eleanor expected. Her tailbone felt bruised by all the jolting, each bump a sharp pain, increasing her impatience. About an hour out of Barrow, a speaker crackled overhead.

"Dr. Marcus, we're approaching Polaris Station. ETA five minutes."

Dr. Marcus sat forward. "We should put our masks back on."

Polaris? That wasn't the name of her mother's research station.

Five minutes later, the transport came to a halt. The driver emerged from the cockpit and came back through their compartment to the outer hatch.

"Hope the ride wasn't too rough," he said, opening it.

"No," Eleanor lied, and ducked through.

What she saw outside the transport stunned her. Polaris Station loomed in the midst of the storm, and it looked like something that belonged on the moon. Three silver pods, each a sphere as big as a house, perched a dozen feet high on six legs, with skeletal feet. Across the surfaces of the spheres, circular windows glowed with their interior light. Elevated tunnels connected the pods, while behind them, a drilling platform towered over the ice sheet, rising up like the black spires of a cathedral.

This was nothing like the research station her mother had described.

Dr. Marcus directed them toward a metal staircase and catwalk that climbed up to an air lock on the nearest pod. Eleanor took the ice-encrusted steps slowly, followed by Luke, then Dr. Marcus. Eleanor tried the outer door but found it locked. Apparently, they didn't follow the Arctic Code out here.

Dr. Marcus slipped past Eleanor and waved her wrist in front of a sensor, and the door opened with a hiss and a clang. They entered the air lock and removed their masks.

"What do you think of Polaris Station?" Dr. Marcus

asked, that perma-smile back in place.

"It's . . . pretty amazing," Eleanor said.

"We have employed the very latest innovations." She made a sweeping game-show-host gesture with her hand. "The pods are equipped with hydraulic legs that lift them up above the rising snow, so they never get buried, and also allow them to relocate, if necessary. Each pod is autonomous and fully mobile. Polaris is able to be wherever we need it to be. And she has *several* even more impressive tricks up her sleeve."

This sounded like the kind of speech she might give to one of those visiting foreign dignitaries.

"My mom worked here?" Eleanor asked.

"We recently incorporated your mother's old facility into Polaris Station. Not the structure, of course, which was woefully outdated, but the staff and the work they were doing." She opened the inner door and extended her usher's hand. "Shall we?"

Eleanor's unease grew. "Incorporated?" she asked, moving slowly toward the opening. This was not what she had expected.

"Sure," Luke said. "Incorporated. You know, the way I *incorporated* my breakfast."

"Speaking of which," Dr. Marcus said, apparently choosing to ignore the barb in Luke's comment, "are either of you hungry?"

Eleanor had grown agitated with the guided tour and the hostess act. "Dr. Marcus," she said, "the only thing I want is to find my mom." She ducked through the door and entered an entirely white hallway. The floor, the ceiling, the walls. Farther ahead, the hallway seemed to open up into a central chamber, also white, where Eleanor glimpsed the base of a chromed spiral staircase.

"Of course you do." Dr. Marcus stepped through. "My apologies. Let's proceed directly to the command module so we can brief you." Her pace quickened down the hallway, for which Eleanor was grateful.

They reached the chamber with the staircase, and Eleanor now saw that it corkscrewed straight up through the center of the sphere, all the way to the top, giving access to the levels above them. The three of them mounted the staircase, swinging around and around.

"This level holds the laboratories," Dr. Marcus said, with less enthusiasm than before, as they reached the first level up. Glass doors and walls encircled the staircase, and through them Eleanor saw banks of computers, monitors, and other equipment. They kept going up.

"Living quarters are found on this level," she said. A ring of smooth, white pocket doors surrounded the staircase, each equipped with a sensor like the one that had admitted them into the pod. A few of the doors had curled newspaper clippings and *Far Side* cartoons taped to them. One door bore the obligatory Einstein-sticking-out-his-tongue photo, while another had a sign that simply said YOU'RE HOT.

"Where is everybody?" Luke asked.

That was a good question. Where were all the researchers and workers the Polaris Station had *incorporated*?

"The command module," Dr. Marcus said. "On the next level, you'll find the kitchen, showers, and recreational space. Above that, on the top level, you'll find the communications systems, along with the various atmospheric sensors, radars, and satellite dishes."

They left the spiral staircase at the kitchen, a cramped area made entirely of stainless steel. Dr. Marcus led them through an adjacent dining area and brought them to one of the elevated tunnels that connected the pods to one another. It looked to be about twenty or thirty feet long, and smaller in diameter than it had appeared from the ground outside.

"I hope you don't mind crawling," Dr. Marcus said. "The command module is in the next pod."

Luke shrugged. "I've been in tighter spots."

Eleanor climbed headfirst into the tunnel, moving

along a rubber track on her hands and knees. The tunnel's shell seemed thinner than that of the sphere— Eleanor could once again hear the wind shrieking on all sides.

When she reached the end, she realized quickly there wouldn't be a graceful way to exit the tunnel. She ended up just kind of slithering out of it to the ground. Luke followed in much the same way, but Dr. Marcus took the extra effort to turn herself around inside the tunnel, with little grunts, and emerge feetfirst.

"This way," she said, smoothing her hair. She led them through a near mirror image of the pod from which they'd just come, except when they reached the laboratory level, they found it replaced by a command center.

Giant screens paneled the walls, displaying maps, charts, and satellite images, while near them, a few whiteboards crawled with indecipherable scientist handwriting. Around the staircase, a dozen or so men and women sat at several rows of computer terminals in fixed swivel chairs. Beyond them, a man stood with his back to Eleanor, staring at one of the maps.

Dr. Marcus called to him. "Sir?"

He turned around, and Eleanor stopped. She'd seen this man hundreds of times. But only once in person.

"Dr. Skinner?" she said.

"Yes," he said. "You must be the intrepid Eleanor Perry."

His voice sounded exactly the same as in the interviews and press conferences he gave on the news, deep and soothing. In many ways, the voice of the Freeze. He stepped toward them, hand outstretched.

"It is a delight to meet you, Miss Perry. And Mr. Fournier, I don't think I've yet had the privilege of thanking you in person for your efforts on behalf of the company."

"Well, I appreciate the work," Luke said. "There's been a lot of it recently."

Eleanor hadn't quite brought her thoughts around to the reality of this. *Dr. Skinner?* Here in this remote outpost at the top of the world? This was the man who had discovered the coming ice age. His presence did explain why Dr. Marcus the Diplomat was there, but what was the CEO of the G.E.T., one of the most powerful men on the planet, doing there in the first place? Eleanor's first thought was that he might be there for her mom, but the G.E.T. had thousands of employees around the world; why would—

"Has Dr. Marcus given you the tour?" Dr. Skinner asked. "What do you think of the place?"

"Mighty impressive," Luke said, looking around and nodding.

Dr. Skinner leaned in with a conspiratorial smirk. "If you ask me, they leaned a bit heavily on the space-colony school of design."

Eleanor couldn't help smiling to hear Dr. Skinner echo her own first impression at seeing the station.

Luke actually chuckled, too. "You might say that."

"But enough pleasantries," Dr. Skinner said. "You are here for your mother, and that's probably the only thing you care about right now."

"Yes," Eleanor said, grateful that he understood what Dr. Marcus hadn't.

"Well, as you can see," Dr. Skinner said, "we're doing everything we can to locate her and Dr. Powers."

"Dr. Powers?" Eleanor asked.

"Yes, another of our top geologists. He and your mother had set out on the ice when we lost contact with them, and we found they hadn't logged their destination. Ordinarily, we would have people out on the ice searching right now, but during the storm, we're having to work remotely, using every resource the company has at its disposal." He indicated the men and women sitting at the computers. "Satellites, radar, thermal imaging. Our team here is scouring the available data, looking for any clue."

"Thank you." Eleanor took a deep breath. All these people were trying to find her mom. But they were

G.E.T. scientists. Eleanor had planned to somehow use the information on her Sync to find her mom, but had no idea how she could do so now without revealing it.

Dr. Skinner cleared his throat. "On the subject of data and clues, Miss Perry, I believe you are in possession of the twin to your mother's Sync?"

Eleanor's body went rigid within her polar gear. "I was."

"Was?" Dr. Skinner said.

"I . . . left my Sync in Phoenix."

"Really?" He turned to Dr. Marcus.

She shook her head, her hair swinging like tassels. "Her uncle couldn't find it at the house."

"I hid it," Eleanor said. "I didn't want anyone taking it."

"That's understandable," Dr. Skinner said. "It's the only connection you have with your mother. Isn't that right?" He didn't wait for an answer. "But it may also contain data that could help us locate her. When was the last time she contacted you?"

"Um . . ." Eleanor decided to omit the later, secret messages. "It was three nights ago."

"Three nights." Dr. Skinner nodded. "Let's see, that would have been the night before she and Dr. Powers left on their expedition. We lost contact with them the next day, their first out on the ice. What did she say to you?"

"Just normal mom stuff," Eleanor said.

"Have you found anything?" Luke asked. "Any sign of them?"

Dr. Skinner nodded. "Yesterday, we located the site of a camp they had made. But what we found was . . . perplexing."

"What was it?" Eleanor asked.

"The camp was empty but undisturbed. It appeared that your mother and Dr. Powers abandoned the site in a matter of moments. Dr. Powers had quit a log entry midsentence. They left their tent behind, along with their food and much of their gear."

"In this storm?" Luke said. "But that's suici—" He shut his mouth without finishing the word, but the seed had already been planted. An aggressive dread quickly took root in Eleanor, a growth of suffocating questions and doubts.

Without a tent, food, and gear, how could her mom have possibly survived on the ice sheet the last few days? Or in this storm? Why had she abandoned her camp?

What could possibly have made her that desperate?

143

⟜ CHAPTER ⟞
12

"MISS PERRY," DR. SKINNER SAID, "WHERE DID YOU hide the Sync?"

Eleanor glanced up to find everyone looking at her. She'd become lost in her fears. "Sorry, Dr. Skinner, what was that?"

Dr. Skinner closed his eyes. "I know how upsetting this must all be. Especially after the ordeal I imagine you went through getting here. But I need you to think, all right? Every moment counts."

"Okay," Eleanor said.

"Good girl." Dr. Skinner smiled. "You said you hid your Sync. I need you to tell me where it is."

"It's . . ." Eleanor had started to sweat inside her

polar gear. She had to bluff something. If she didn't give a convincing answer, they'd know she was lying, and they might even figure out that she had the Sync with her. "It's at my school."

Dr. Skinner frowned. "What, in your locker?"

"No. I didn't want anyone to find it, so I hid it where they're doing the construction."

A flash of irritation, and perhaps even anger, crossed Dr. Skinner's eyes. "Your Sync is hidden at a *construction* site?"

"Yes."

"Where, exactly?" Dr. Skinner asked.

Dr. Marcus had pulled out a small notepad, her pen poised to write.

"There's an air duct near a fire hose," Eleanor said. Off to her side, she heard the scratch of Dr. Marcus's pen. "I pulled off the grate and stuck the Sync inside."

"Thank you, Miss Perry." Dr. Skinner gave a quick nod to Dr. Marcus, who nodded back and left the command module. Dr. Skinner patted the side of Eleanor's shoulder. "We'll have someone retrieve that shortly. And as soon as we can, we'll return it to you. I know how important it must be to you."

Unlike Dr. Marcus, who said the wrong things at the wrong time, Dr. Skinner said the right things, even if they still somehow managed to *feel* wrong. But he

145

sounded just right enough for Eleanor to wonder if she was being too paranoid. What if the Sync really could help find her mom? Wasn't that worth it, no matter what her mom had told her to do?

The building heat in her gear shortened her breath. "Dr. Skinner?"

"Yes?"

She was about to tell him the truth. She wanted to. But she remembered what Felipe had said.

I'm telling you. Something is going on.

With the G.E.T. mobilizing up here the way they seemed to be, and ghost wolves and Inupiat sleds out on the ice, her mom going missing, inexplicably abandoning her camp, the secret messages she had sent . . . Eleanor needed to know more before she said or did something she might later regret.

"Miss Perry?" Dr. Skinner asked.

"I—I just appreciate everything you're doing to find my mom."

"No thanks are necessary. We take care of our own." He paused. "Was that all you wanted to say?"

"Yes."

He looked at her for an uncomfortable moment in which she tried to keep her expression blank. "Very well," he said at last. "I'm sure you're tired. Our transports are not known for their comfort. We have a room

146

for you in the next pod where you can remove your gear and stow your pack. You too, Mr. Fournier."

Luke tipped his head. "Much obliged. Though I hope I won't enjoy your hospitality for long. I plan to fly out as soon as the storm breaks."

At that point, Dr. Marcus returned from wherever she'd been. Another nod passed between her and Dr. Skinner, and Eleanor felt certain that in that very moment, someone from the G.E.T. was speeding toward her high school.

"Oh," Dr. Skinner said. "And I suspect you'll want to meet Finn and Julian."

"Who?" Eleanor asked.

"Dr. Powers's sons," Dr. Skinner said. "They're staying in the next pod as well."

Dr. Powers had brought his sons up here to the Arctic? Eleanor's mom had always said it was no place for children, every time Eleanor had asked if she could come visit.

"Right this way, please." Dr. Marcus gestured with her usher's hand again, and her hostess polish returned. "I think you'll find your living quarters to be *very* comfortable."

Eleanor rolled her eyes, and she and Luke followed the woman up the staircase from the command module to a second tunnel. This one led to the last of the three pods, and Eleanor traversed it in the same way she had the first.

On the other side, Dr. Marcus led Eleanor and Luke to the living quarters and gave them each a key card to the sensors on their doors. Eleanor tried hers, and the door slid away with a gentle whoosh. Inside her narrow room, she found a small desk against the pod's outer wall, with a circular window above it. To the right of the desk were two beds, each within its own private alcove, one stacked atop the other. Each alcove had a bright lamp recessed in its ceiling. They looked like tanning beds.

"Those lights are full spectrum," Dr. Marcus said. "We prescribe mandatory time under them to maintain vitamin D levels and emotional health in our staff."

Eleanor nodded. Her mother had complained about both of those problems at her previous facility.

"I'll leave you alone a moment to change and stow your equipment." Dr. Marcus swiped her hand in front of the sensor, and the door whooshed closed. Eleanor went to it and peered through the door's window, hoping for a bit more privacy, especially with Dr. Powers's boys running around. She noticed a button beneath the window. When she pressed it, the window turned opaque.

Eleanor marveled for a moment and then quickly

peeled herself out of her gear, down to her underwear. The air of the pod hit her skin like a cool shower, and she sighed for a moment in relief from the heat. But a few moments later, her skin raised in goose bumps, and she noticed a pair of loose-fitting gray sweatpants and a sweatshirt folded neatly on her bed. She figured they were for her and put them on. Next, she had to figure out what she would do with her Sync. She wasn't about to leave it unattended in her room. Dr. Marcus had a key.

Eleanor reached into her pack and pulled out the device. The only safe place would be with her, so she slipped the Sync into one of her pants pockets. The sweatshirt was baggy enough to hide its presence. Then she stepped out of her room. Dr. Marcus and Luke were waiting for her.

"Ah, wonderful. I believe Julian and Finn are upstairs having lunch," Dr. Marcus said. "Would you care to join them?"

"Yes," Eleanor said.

She and Luke followed Dr. Marcus up the spiral staircase to the pod's kitchen. Two boys sat at a table, one of them laughing, the other not. The one laughing appeared older, about sixteen, with deep-brown skin and green eyes, his black hair shaved close. His younger, much skinnier brother, who looked about

Eleanor's age, wore his hair a bit longer but had the same green eyes. Both wore the same gray sweatpants and sweatshirt Eleanor did.

"Julian, Finn," Dr. Marcus called. "I'd like you to meet Eleanor Perry and Luke Fournier."

The Powers brothers looked up. The older one smiled.

"Which one of you is which?" Luke asked, reaching out his hand.

"I'm Julian," the older one said, returning Luke's solid shake. "This is Finn."

"I can introduce myself," Finn said.

"Sorry," Julian said. "This is Finn, who will introduce himself at some point."

Finn narrowed his eyes.

"And you're Eleanor?" Julian asked. He spoke like a coach. "Dr. Perry's daughter?"

"Yes," Eleanor said.

Dr. Marcus brought her hands together. "Well, now that introductions have been made, I have work I must attend to. I'll leave you all here to get further acquainted. There's a video game console for your diversion. So, relax and settle in."

Relax?

She swept from the room, leaving the four of them alone.

"Have a seat," Julian said, motioning Eleanor and Luke to their table. "You just got in, right?"

"Yeah," Eleanor said. "We were in Barrow last night."

Julian shook his head. "That place is crazy. I heard you came up here alone?"

"Um." Eleanor tipped her head back and forth. "Sort of."

"What she means," Luke said, "is that she stowed away on my plane and wouldn't even be here talking to you boys if it weren't for me."

"Yes, Luke," Eleanor said. "That's what I meant." She looked at Finn, who still hadn't said much of anything. "What about you guys?"

"Our dad sent for us," Julian said. "We were with our mom in Florida. That's where she moved after they got divorced. We were supposed to get here the day before our dad disappeared, but they kept delaying our flight."

"Your dad sent for you?" Eleanor asked. "Here? To the *Arctic*?"

Julian shrugged. "Sure. He takes us everywhere. It just depends."

"On what?" Eleanor asked.

"Whether he can convince our mother to let us go," Finn said. His voice was quieter than his brother's, but no less confident. "If you knew our mother, you would know how difficult that can be."

"And she agreed to let you come to the Arctic?" Eleanor asked.

Julian and Finn looked at each other, a momentary glance. They had that sibling thing going, and Eleanor suspected each knew what the other was thinking most of the time. She felt like she had that with her mom, sometimes.

"We didn't exactly tell her," Julian said.

"We lied and told her we were going somewhere else." Finn folded his arms. "Somewhere she wouldn't worry about us."

"Where would that be?" Luke asked.

"Venezuela," Finn said.

"She's figured it out now, though." Julian chuckled, shaking his head. "And believe me, I am *not* looking forward to going home to face *that*."

Finn glared at his older brother. "Really? That's what you're worried about?"

Eleanor did find Julian's cavalier attitude a bit odd. His dad was missing. In the middle of a polar storm, just like Eleanor's mom.

"Relax, bro." Julian kept his smile in place, even as his tone fell a note. "Just trying to keep you from dragging us all down."

Finn raised his voice, as if to counterbalance his

brother's. "I believe the situation is what's dragging you down, *bro*. Not me."

"Now I know you two are brothers," Luke said.

"Whatever." Julian rose from the table. "I'm going to my room."

"*Our* room," Finn said.

"Not for the next hour, if you know what's good for you." With that, Julian stalked out of the kitchen and went downstairs.

Silence followed. Eleanor decided to just let it settle and leave it alone until Finn chose to disturb it, which he did a few moments later.

"Have they found anything?" he asked.

Eleanor shook her head.

"Dr. Marcus said you've been communicating with your mom through a Sync." He raised his eyebrows, making that a question.

"Yeah, I have," Eleanor said.

"So they can use that to find them, right? They said they can use that."

"I, uh, left it back home."

His eyebrows fell together into a scowl. "Why would you do that?"

"Excuse me?" Eleanor narrowed her eyes. "This happens to be my first trip to the North freaking Pole. I didn't exactly think this was the safest place to bring an irreplaceable piece of technology."

Finn leaned back and said, "Whatever," sounding just like his older brother had.

Eleanor snorted. "Don't whatever me."

"Well, this is fun." Luke slapped the table with both hands. "But I'm gonna follow Julian's lead and head to my room." With that, he leaned on his hands and rose from the table, then strolled out of the kitchen and down the spiral stairs, leaving Eleanor and Finn alone.

"You can go, too," he said a moment later.

Eleanor wasn't about to let him think he'd told her what to do. She also knew he was only acting this way because he was scared for his dad. Like she was for her mom. So she stayed.

"They're going to find them," she said.

"You don't know that."

"And you don't know they won't. So why not believe what you want to believe?"

He seemed to be thinking about that, but then he shook his head. "I can't just . . . ignore the odds like that."

"My mom says human beings are terrible at figuring odds. If we were better at it, we'd never get in a car."

Finn looked up, a half grin on his face. "I guess that's true."

"Of course it's true," Eleanor said. "And I'm glad

you can admit when you're wrong."

He looked like he was about to argue that but decided to let it go. "I really got my hopes up about your Sync," he said.

Eleanor lowered her gaze to the almost imperceptible bulge beneath her sweatshirt and then moved it to the table, studying the fingerprints on the stainless steel. "I'm sorry." For a moment, she thought about letting him in on the secret, but she decided against it. Not until she knew whether he'd go running to Skinner. Of course, very soon the G.E.T. would realize her Sync wasn't hidden at the school, and Eleanor didn't know what she would do then.

"Sometimes—" Finn started. "Sometimes I feel like they're keeping something from us. Like they know something."

Eleanor realized she had felt that way since arriving at Polaris Station, too. She had assumed that suspicion arose from the texts her mom had sent, but if Finn had also sensed it, perhaps there was something else to it.

"I feel the same way," she said. "What are the odds of that?"

Eleanor spent the next few hours playing video games with Finn, and then Julian came back upstairs. He gave a single nod to Finn and Eleanor as he entered the kitchen. Finn nodded back, and Eleanor decided that was probably their way of making up.

"You hungry, Ellie?" Julian asked. "Mind if I call you Ellie?"

"Nope, that's what all my friends call me. And yes, I'm hungry."

"Well, you've got a whole two flavors of instant ramen to choose from," he said. "They make dinners in the evening, but during the day we're on our own, and everything here is dehydrated. Want me to boil you some water?"

"Sure," she said, but before the kettle whistled, Dr. Skinner came up the stairs.

"Miss Perry, may I speak with you a moment?"

Eleanor's appetite fled, and her stomach turned on her. It was about the Sync—she knew it. Finn and Julian watched as she got up from the table and followed Dr. Skinner down the stairs. They reached the living quarters, and he gave them a look around.

"Are you satisfied with your room?" he asked.

That wasn't what he had come to ask, but the question was unexpected, so it tipped her a bit off balance. "Uh, sure. Yeah, it's great."

"I'm pleased." But then he sighed. "We had someone go to your school."

Silence followed. She wondered if he expected her to fill it.

"They could not locate your Sync," he said.

"WHAT?" Eleanor had wanted her shock to sound genuine, but even to her own ear, it sounded forced. "What do you mean? That's where I left it!"

"My people tell me the location was not at all secure," Dr. Skinner said. "Honestly, I can't imagine what you must have been thinking to hide it there."

"I don't know, I didn't have a lot of time, I just had to—"

"You are *certain* that is where you placed it?"

She nodded. "Yes, sir." She meant it to be convincing, but Dr. Skinner's stare hardened. "I'm certain," Eleanor added.

"Then we must consider that asset lost. Miss Perry, I must tell you, without your Sync, our chances of locating your mother have diminished greatly."

Eleanor restrained her anger. Was he trying to make her feel guilty? Was it a ploy? Was he trying to flush out her deception? Did he expect her to just cave and whip it out?

"I'm sorry," she whispered.

"Don't apologize to me. Apologize to your mother." He turned away. "*If* we find her, that is."

⊸ CHAPTER ⊸
13

If? THAT WORD CUT RIGHT TO THE CENTER OF ELEANOR'S chest as cleanly as the icy air, and she nearly gasped.

"Hey, Skinner!" Luke charged out of his room. "What's your problem, talking to her like that?"

Dr. Skinner looked back. "I said nothing untrue."

"That ain't the point!" Luke shouted. "You got no call to speak to her that way!"

"May I remind you that I am—"

"I don't care who you are! She's just a kid!"

Eleanor appreciated that Luke was defending her, but she was afraid of what Dr. Skinner could do to his cargo business. Besides, she was the one who was hiding something.

"Mr. Fournier," Dr. Skinner said, "feelings do not matter, not even those of Miss Perry, young as she is. What is important right now is finding Dr. Perry and Dr. Powers. What is important is the continued health and success of my company. What is important is the continued health and success of our species. *Those* are things that matter." He glanced at Eleanor. "She may indulge whatever emotions she chooses. I won't waste my time and energy on such concerns. Now if you'll excuse me, I have two missing scientists to locate."

He walked away toward the tunnel to the command module.

"I really don't like that guy," Luke said.

Eleanor was angry, too, but this was all because of her lie, and she didn't like to see Luke so worked up on behalf of it. "It's okay," she said. "I don't care what he says."

"Good," he said. "Because your mom will turn up. No matter what that corporate TV personality says."

Eleanor smiled. "Thanks, Luke. And thanks for coming out here to the station with me."

"Beats sleeping on Felipe's floor," he said.

"Ellie?" Julian called down the staircase.

"Yeah?"

"Ramen's done."

Eleanor and Luke climbed back up to the dining area. Eleanor sat down to a steaming bowl, and Luke slid into the booth next to her. Julian and Finn sat across from them, each with a bowl as well. The underdone noodles were a little crunchy, but the salty broth tasted good.

"We overheard some of what Skinner was saying to you," Finn said.

"Yeah." Julian slurped up a mouthful of noodles and then spoke through them as he chewed. "That guy sucks. That's our dad out there, too."

Julian didn't sound as concerned for his dad as Eleanor felt for her mom. "How worried are you guys?" she asked. "Really?"

Finn and Julian looked at each other. Julian pushed his nearly empty bowl aside.

"I'm worried," Julian said. "We're worried. We just try not to think about it, you know?"

Finn poked at his noodles with his fork. "*Julian* tries not to think about it."

"There's just no point in getting all worked up about it," Julian said. "There's nothing we can do. We're stuck in here. We just have to wait."

Eleanor didn't feel that way, and she didn't think she could just not think about her mom being lost out there. There *was* something she could do. With the information her mom had sent. She just needed to find out what it meant without revealing the Sync to anyone.

Later that evening, Dr. Marcus returned to invite them all over to the next pod for dinner. When Eleanor reached the dining room, she found it crowded with what must have been every scientist and crew member of Polaris Station. Now that everyone was gathered here in one place, Eleanor tried to see if she recognized any of her mother's previous coworkers. She had seen photos, and even met a few of them, but so far everyone in that mess hall looked unfamiliar.

She took a table with Luke and the Powers brothers, plates of reconstituted beef stroganoff in front of them, while Dr. Skinner addressed the room.

"Good work today," Dr. Skinner said over the clattering of utensils against plastic bowls. "Tomorrow, we'll concentrate our efforts on sector H9-11. After we're done here, let's recalibrate and set our new parameters. Enjoy your dinner." He sat down.

Eleanor finally spotted a man she recognized, over in a corner, eating by himself. She thought he was Dr. Grant, the one Uncle Jack had called a few days ago.

"Be right back," she whispered to Luke, and left her seat. She ducked across the room, weaving between chairs and tables, until she reached the corner. He looked up from his food as she approached and wiped his mouth with a crinkly paper napkin.

"Oh," he said. "Eleanor, isn't it?"

"Yes, Dr. Grant. You work with my mom—"

"Yes, yes, of course, I remember you. I'm so glad you're safe and sound." He pointed to an empty chair. "Please, sit down."

Eleanor took the seat he offered. "Did you find anything today?"

"Um . . ." He shook his head. "Not today, no. I'm so sorry. But we'll keep looking, don't you worry."

Eleanor hadn't really expected him to tell her anything new. "Where is everyone else from Sohn International?"

He looked around. "I'm all that's left of the old gang, I'm afraid. Everyone else has been reassigned. We're part of the Global Energy Trust now."

"Yeah, my uncle Jack mentioned some big project. When you talked with him—"

"That's right, Jack called the old satellite phone." Dr. Grant wiped his mouth again. "You know, I found out later I wasn't even supposed to have that old thing." He leaned in, a conspiratorial hand shielding his mouth. "Truth be told, I actually got in a bit of trouble for talking with your uncle. All these new protocols and procedures. But I'm lucky to have my job, and it's always that way working for a new company, I suppose."

"Uh, I guess."

"Well, it's good to see you alive and well. We were worried, you know. But I, uh, see your friends over there. Julian, Finn. They're probably missing you, so . . ." He glanced across the room, and his voice just trailed off.

Missing her? No, Dr. Grant was trying to get rid of her. Maybe he was afraid to talk to her after getting in trouble over Uncle Jack. Regardless, she had to ask one more question.

"What was the big project?"

Dr. Grant opened his mouth as if to speak. A moment went by. "It, uh—" He glanced over Eleanor's shoulder, and in a flash his whole demeanor shriveled. "Hello, Dr. Skinner," he said.

Eleanor looked behind her as Dr. Skinner walked up to their table. Whatever Dr. Grant was about to say, he wouldn't say it now.

"Dr. Grant," Skinner said. "I see you're acquainted with Miss Perry."

"Yes." Dr. Grant nodded toward Eleanor. "I was just telling her how grateful we all are that she's safe."

"Very grateful, indeed," Dr. Skinner said. "Miss

163

Perry, would you mind joining me in the command module? I would like your assistance."

"Um, okay." Eleanor didn't want to go anywhere with him, at least not alone. Not after the way he had treated her last time. "Can Finn come?"

Dr. Skinner's face remained impassive. "I suppose, if you feel it necessary." He walked away between the tables.

Dr. Grant smiled at Eleanor as she left him alone at his table. She crossed the kitchen, and on her way past Finn, she tapped him on the shoulder. "Come on."

He got up and followed her without asking for an explanation. Julian looked a bit puzzled but stayed seated. Luke dug back into his meal.

Eleanor and Finn met Dr. Skinner by the staircase, and down they went to the command module, where the giant screens blinked with their changing maps and charts.

"After your failure to produce the Sync"—Dr. Skinner led them over to a desk—"I hope you'll be willing to assist me in another way."

"How?" Every time Dr. Skinner mentioned the Sync, Eleanor worried that he somehow knew it was there, in her pocket.

Dr. Skinner pulled a laptop out of a drawer and set it on the desk. He lifted its screen open to reveal a log-in. Eleanor recognized the profile picture, a cat with a tiny pirate patch over one eye.

"That's my mom's computer," she said.

"Yes, it is," Dr. Skinner said.

"Her *personal* computer." That was her mom's private property. But perhaps, if Eleanor could get a look at what it contained, she might find something that would make sense of all this.

"Yes, her personal computer," Dr. Skinner said. "And as such, I have no way to access it. My people have tried and failed to break the security, but I wondered if you—"

"Isn't that illegal?" Finn asked. "Hacking someone's computer?"

Dr. Skinner looked down at him. "When that someone has gone missing, young man, exigent circumstances prevail over privacy."

Eleanor actually remembered the password, unless her mom had changed it, but she wasn't just going to give it to Skinner. "Why do you need to break into her laptop?"

Dr. Skinner sighed. "Miss Perry, though I cannot fathom why, I'm starting to believe that you are being deliberately oppositional. I am trying to find your mother." He pointed at the laptop. "To that end, I am pursuing every lead available to me."

Eleanor swallowed. No matter what he said, or how rational he made it sound, she had no intention of giving him what he wanted. Her mother's last message flashed in her mind: *Show no one.*

But she said, "Okay," and placed her hands on the keyboard.

She typed in several random words, quickly, so Dr. Skinner wouldn't see what they were.

"Rock Canyon?" he asked.

Okay, so he was fast. "It was a password she used back at home."

"It didn't work. Try something else."

Eleanor moved on, faking her way through half a dozen attempts. She noticed Finn had moved away and was studying one of the giant screens. After a few tries, she finally said, "I'm sorry, Dr. Skinner. I don't think I know it."

He slammed the lid closed on the laptop, almost catching her fingers. "You continue to disappoint, Miss Perry. We are running out of time and options. If by chance some inspiration strikes you, let us try again. For now, you are free to return to your pod."

"Yes, sir."

"You too, Mr. Powers." Dr. Skinner looked at Finn. "Yes, sir."

The two of them left Skinner in the command

module and climbed back up to the dining area. Most of the scientists and crew members had left, Eleanor assumed to their sleeping quarters in the first pod. Luke and Julian were gone, too, so Eleanor and Finn climbed through the tunnel to the third pod and found them waiting at a table in their kitchen.

"What was that all about?" Julian asked as Finn and Eleanor took a seat.

"He wanted the password to break into my mom's laptop," Eleanor said.

"Did you give it to him?" Julian asked.

"She faked it," Finn said. "Even I could tell."

"Listen, kid." Luke dragged both his hands down his stubbly face. "These guys are corporate suits, I'll give you that, and I don't trust Skinner any further than I can throw him. But he's not some evil mastermind. He's just trying to keep you and your uncle from suing the pants off his company. He's in damage control here. If you know something, you might want to help them out."

"I can't," Eleanor said. "*We* have to do something."

"Like what?" Julian asked.

Eleanor leaned toward them across the table and lowered her voice. "What if we could find information about where they were, and we went out to search for them on our own?"

"Out on the ice sheet?" Julian asked. "You're crazy."

"I'll see your crazy and raise you a stupid," Luke said.

Finn gave Eleanor a nod. "I'll go."

"What?" Julian swiveled to his younger brother. "No way. Mom would kill us!"

"Then don't come," Finn said. "I don't care. They're not doing anything to find Dad."

"Sure they are," Luke said. "They're sending out search parties, and right now there's a whole lot of people in the next"—he flapped his hand toward the tunnel—"pod thing, and they're all working—"

"They're not searching for our parents," Finn said.

Julian leaned back in his seat, away from his brother. "This again."

"What do you mean, Finn?" Eleanor asked.

"It's just—" Finn dropped his voice low. "I don't think—okay, they *are* searching for our parents, but they're not trying to find them."

"I'm confused," Luke said. "Doesn't that amount to the same thing?"

Finn shook his head. "I think they're really just trying to find what our parents were working on." He pressed his index finger into the table, as if marking the spot on a map. "But the only way to do that is to find our parents."

Julian and Luke both wore competing scowls, but they seemed to be listening. When Eleanor thought about all the secret files her mom had sent her, and added that to what Finn had just said, it started to make sense why Skinner seemed so desperate to get her Sync, and now her laptop. It was as Eleanor had suspected. It wasn't about finding her mom. The G.E.T. wanted those files.

"All right, for the sake of argument," Luke said, "where'd you get this idea?"

"While Eleanor was typing fake passwords," Finn said, "I got a closer look at one of the computer screens. They're searching for energy signatures."

Julian tipped his head up toward the ceiling. "Of course they are—"

"No," Finn said. "Not an energy signature like what our parents would make. They're looking for something bigger than that. Much bigger. A telluric signature."

Telluric. That word sat Eleanor upright in her seat. "Luke, your plane was full of telluric equipment."

Luke nodded.

"What does telluric even mean?" Julian asked.

"I looked it up," Eleanor said. "It just means earth."

"Yes and no," Finn said. "Telluric currents are supposedly these bands of energy that crisscross the

169

earth, under the surface." He turned to Julian. "Dad's talked about them."

"He has?" Julian asked.

"If you ever paid attention," Finn said, with a hint of smugness in his voice. "Some people call them ley lines. They supposedly produce massive amounts of energy. But these are, like, crackpot theories, right? Really fringe stuff. I didn't think anyone believed in them."

"So why is Skinner looking for them?" Eleanor asked.

"Um," Luke said, "I'm going to venture a guess it has something to do with his running an *energy* company."

Eleanor ignored his sarcasm. Could telluric currents be the large discovery her mother had made? What if the numbers she'd sent had something to do with the energy deposit Skinner wanted to find?

"My point is," Finn said, "Skinner's not in this for our parents. I'm with Eleanor. It's up to us to find them."

"Okay, we're done." Julian stood up. "No more of this. You hear me? No more talking about going out there to search. No more talking about ley lines or whatever they're called. No more. Period. You bring it up again, and I'll go to Skinner myself."

"Julian!" Finn shouted.

"No, Finn, you listen to me! I may not be as smart as you and Dad. I may not know all about computers and ley lines and telluric whatevers, but I am your older brother, and I know a stupid idea when I hear one. Dad is out there, got it? They will find him, and they will bring him home. Our job is to shut up and stay out of their way—or help them, if we can." He shot a look at Eleanor. "Now I'm going to bed. I suggest you do the same."

With that, Eleanor watched Julian storm away for the second time since she'd met him. Luke rose from the table soon after.

"Julian's right," he said. "Skinner's a piece of work, but you kids need to keep yourselves safe above all. I know that's what your parents would want." Then he, too, went downstairs.

Once again, Eleanor found herself alone with Finn. He glowered across the table from her, and she wanted to help but wasn't sure how or what she should say. So she just stayed quiet and waited.

"My brother's not stupid," he finally said.

"I know," Eleanor said.

"He only says that because our dad's a scientist and I get straight As. Like, he doesn't fit in, or something." Finn rubbed his eyes hard. "I shouldn't have said that about him not paying attention."

"You're a good brother. I know what it's like to not fit in. It feels—"

"Let's just go to bed, okay?" Finn labored out of his seat. "I gotta go talk to him before he falls asleep."

"Oh. Okay."

Eleanor got out of her seat and awkwardly followed Finn down the spiral staircase. He trudged to the room he shared with Julian, said, "G'night," and went inside.

"Night," Eleanor said.

She opened her own door and entered her room. At the sight of her bed, an overpowering exhaustion rolled over her, dragging her down. But on her way there, she caught a glimpse through her window. She killed all the lights in her room so she could see better, her nose pressed against the cold, thick glass, breath fogging it up in waves, blades of icy crystal crawling across the outer pane.

White.

So much white.

Barrow was out there somewhere, that lawless, vile place, while the original Barrow lay buried beneath it under miles of ice. If that ice kept up its terrible advance, all the way to the equator, the whole world would look like this one day. This blank nothingness that erased everything. Even with all its advances, how long would Polaris Station last? How long would Barrow, or any place, last?

But then she saw something out there. Something not white. A shadow wavering in and out of the blowing snow. Eleanor squinted, straining to see what could possibly be moving out there, where nothing was supposed to survive. A creeping fear moved along her skin, like an ice sheet claiming her. Perhaps what Felipe had said shaped the image in her mind, but she swore she could see four legs. A thick neck and a tail.

A wolf.

And with that wolf something else. The tall shadowy figure of a man.

CHAPTER
14

ELEANOR BLINKED AND SQUINTED, BUT THE HARDER SHE strained to see them, the more the figures eluded her, until she finally had to admit they were gone, and might never have been there in the first place, a projection of her own imagination onto the void. She wanted to believe that was the explanation, rather than ghost wolves, but couldn't convince herself of it enough to fall asleep. She lay there in her bed, in her narrow room, inside a sphere as inconsequential as a marble tossed into a snowbank.

She kept replaying the night's previous conversations in her mind, treating each piece of information as the part of a larger whole, studying each of them, rotating each of them, trying to fit them all together. Before long, she felt that she had assembled them into something that made at least a little sense.

The best theory that she could come up with was that her mother had recently discovered an energy source, a telluric energy source, and the G.E.T. had come in with their crazy Arctic station and basically taken over. Eleanor's mom and Dr. Powers had then gone out onto the ice sheet, perhaps to do more research, and something had happened. What it was Eleanor didn't know, but what she did know was that whatever her mother found, she had decided to send it to Eleanor to keep it secret and safe. Then she and Dr. Powers had vanished.

Assuming that was all true, Eleanor still needed more information. There were too many gaps and unanswered questions, like the meaning of those files her mom had sent, and that number code. Could they hold the key to finding Mom, as the G.E.T. seemed to think? If so, Eleanor's best chance at finding some of those answers might be her mother's laptop. If she could just get a look at it.

It had been a few hours since she'd gone to bed. The rest of Polaris Station would likely be asleep. If she had any chance of getting a look at the computer unobserved, it was now. She could sneak over to the command module, dig around through the laptop, and put it back before anyone noticed.

Eleanor climbed out of bed and opened the door to her room. The pod had apparently gone into some kind of power save. It was cold enough in the common areas for her breath to become a wisp, and most of the lights were out, rendering the station a dark and frightening maze.

She went barefoot to the tunnel connecting her pod to the command module and paused outside it. A hatch had closed over it, sealing it off. Eleanor found a handle and turned it with a bit of difficulty. The hatch opened with a *clunk*. Inside, the tunnel to the next pod had become a black cave, and even though she knew what lay on the other side, she hesitated before climbing in. After she'd gone a few feet, she heard the hatch swing shut behind her automatically, sealing her in darkness.

The storm hadn't let up at all since the last time she'd crossed the bridge. It ripped around the tunnel, shaking the entire structure. Eleanor, in her sweats and bare feet, without her polar gear, felt more vulnerable to it than she ever had since coming to the Arctic, the closest the cold had come to claiming her. She was shivering within moments and scrambled the rest of the way as quickly as she could.

When she reached the opposite end, she found the

hatch open a crack. She closed it behind her, the pod she emerged into as cold and dark as hers had been. But two levels down the command module glowed fitfully with the activity of its screens and monitors. It was also empty, as she'd hoped it would be.

She skulked, shivering, down the rows of computer terminals to the desk where Dr. Skinner had shown Eleanor her mother's laptop. She found it in the same drawer and lifted the screen to the same familiar log-in. She typed in the password, *EllBell*, and the computer opened itself up.

But now Eleanor had to figure out what she was looking for. She started with a simple search for the word *telluric*. That brought up a few emails between her mom and various scientists in different parts of the world with intriguing subject lines.

Subject: Latent telluric strength . . .

RE: Possibility of telluric concentrations . . .

RE: Subject: Telluric energy currents: static or durable . . .

FW: Loss of telluric energy strength over distance . . .

When she opened these emails to read them, she found they were all more than a year old, mostly just debating whether telluric currents actually exist. Nothing about any sort of discovery. Eleanor's search also brought up a few research papers, but they sounded pretty fringe, as Finn had said. Most were written by the same guy, Dr. Johann von Albrecht. Titles like "Earth Energy: Secret Power of the Ancient World," and "The Great Pyramids: Power Plants of the Pharaohs," and "Did an Energy Crisis Destroy Atlantis?" Pretty out there. Some of the articles even talked about *aliens*. But as far as Eleanor could see, none contained information that pointed to the situation here in the Arctic, so she moved on.

She searched for *Global Energy Trust*, and this brought up a bunch of files, but when Eleanor dove into them, they seemed to mostly consist of legal documents, drilling claims, and accounting ledgers. Poring over them took up quite a bit of time, which Eleanor didn't think she had to waste, but it didn't result in anything useful.

She tried searching *Arctic*, but that brought up more information than she could possibly sift through. Morning was coming, and she had no idea how early Skinner and the others would be up. She needed to try something else but didn't know what.

In one last attempt, she entered the number code

she had memorized from her Sync. That search brought up a single result, an email her mother had sent to Dr. Simon Powers, Finn and Julian's dad.

> Simon,
> I have revisited the site of the coordinates we discussed (70°56'28.24"N 156°53'27.80"W). Since my last expedition, the anomalous energy signature has increased tenfold and appears to be trending upward exponentially. What was first considered a trivial concentration is now a viable energy source, if it can be tapped (though I wouldn't give von Albrecht a Nobel quite yet, ha ha). Would love your presence and input on this project.
> Sincerely,
> Samantha

Coordinates! That answered Eleanor's question about the meaning of the code. The numbers did, in fact, identify the site of the deposit her mother had found. That was what her mother had wanted Eleanor to keep secret. That was what Skinner really wanted, just as Finn had said.

The email was dated several months ago. When

Eleanor did a search for any additional messages to Dr. Powers, she found nothing. Apparently, her mother didn't use this laptop much.

A harsh light flashed on overhead, and Eleanor flinched. She looked around in a panic, but it seemed to have turned on automatically. Another light flared, and another, and another, dominoing through the command module. The pod was waking up.

Eleanor deleted the email, signed out of her mother's log-in, and closed the lid. Then she replaced the laptop in the desk drawer and hurried back to the tunnel. She wasn't looking forward to this, but she turned the handle, opened the hatch, and climbed in. The hatch swung shut behind her with a *clunk*, and she started the frigid crossing.

Those coordinates, that site her mom had discovered. They were the keys. She assumed that was where her mother and Dr. Powers had been going when they vanished, and now she knew for certain that would be the place to begin a search for them. For now, only Eleanor had this information, and she had to get there, somehow.

Her limbs trembled from the cold of the tunnel. Her toes and fingers hurt. But she reached the far side and . . .

There was no handle.

Eleanor blinked at the hatch. She thought back. The command module hatch had already been open when she'd reached it. How had she not checked to make sure they opened from both sides? How could she have been that stupid?

She willed herself not to panic but failed a few moments in. She was trapped in a tunnel suspended between two Arctic pods, above the ice sheet, in the middle of a polar storm. She wore a pair of sweats, had no shoes, and it was cold enough in here for hypothermia to set in if she didn't get out soon.

How long until someone opened the tunnel from the other side? It was getting difficult to breathe, both from the cold and the racing of her own heart. She could die in here. The cold had found her. It had waited, biding its time, to seize the first opportunity of weakness she gave it.

For the next few minutes, she banged on the hatch, hoping to wake Luke, Finn, or Julian. But no one came. It was still early, and they were sleeping in their rooms, their doors closed, one level down, unable to hear her.

Her teeth chattered so hard her jaw ached. She tucked her legs up tight and pulled her arms inside her sweatshirt, hugging herself in the fetal position. She had to conserve the heat at her core.

Minutes went by. She didn't know how many. Her whole body began to numb, and she knew what that meant. The fact that it didn't feel as cold anymore terrified her, but soon, that fear gave way to a blurring of her thoughts. Through her fog, Eleanor knew these were all very, very bad signs.

She roused what energy she had and banged on the hatch again. "Help!" she shouted, her voice echoing weakly back and forth from one end of the tunnel to the other. "Help me! Luke! Finn! Anybody!"

Still no one came.

She slumped against the hatch, drained of energy. The storm seemed to be laughing at her outside the tunnel. A savage, pitiless laugh. She closed her eyes, and that laugh filled her, its icy disdain echoing through her bones.

Something clunked near her head. The hatch fell away, and Eleanor fell with it, right out of the tunnel.

"Hold on," a voice said. "I gotcha."

Eleanor felt hot hands grabbing her. She looked up as someone lowered her gently to the ground. It was Finn.

The worry on his face roused fear back into her. "Be right back," he whispered.

Eleanor already felt a bit warmer there, lying on the floor. But she felt even warmer when a moment later Finn returned with a thermal blanket.

"There," he said, tucking it in around her. "You're going to be fine."

"Finn?" Eleanor felt the warmth of the blanket charging inward, driving out the storm, waging a painful battle for her muscles and bones.

"I'm here," he said, rubbing her shoulders with both hands.

She winced. "Thank you."

"Not a problem," he said. "I'll make you wait to tell me what you were doing in there."

Eleanor felt the fog burning away from her mind. She blinked. "My mom's laptop."

"What about it?"

"I opened it up." Eleanor's leg and arm muscles spasmed, coming back to life. "I know what my mom was after. With your dad. I know what Skinner is after."

"You do?" Finn asked.

Eleanor nodded, letting her eyes close. "And I know where to find it."

A short while later, Eleanor sat at one of the tables in the kitchen with a hot bowl of undercooked ramen, the blanket still wrapped around her. Finn and Julian sat across from her while Luke paced the small space.

"Pretty dumb move, kid." His voice was even, but

Eleanor could tell he was angry.

She found she was even a little angry with herself, but she wasn't about to let him know that. "Was it, Luke? What are you, my dad now? And I would have been fine if the doors had actually opened from inside, like pretty much every other door in the world."

"They do," Julian said. "But the outer doors only open by key card. For security."

"Oh." Eleanor felt the key card she had in her pocket. The key card that had been in her pocket the entire time. She bowed her head, embarrassed, but also reminded of what a simple mistake up here could mean. "How did you know I was in there, anyway?" she asked Finn.

"I heard you banging," he said.

"What if he hadn't?" Luke asked. "You'd be dead. You know that, right?"

"Yes, Luke." A shiver grabbed Eleanor by the spine. "I'm well aware of that."

"No, I really don't think you are." He stopped pacing and came to lean over her, his knuckles on the table. "I saved you once. Finn saved you this time. What happens next time, if one of us isn't around?"

"Hopefully, there won't be a next time," she said. "But it doesn't matter. I came up here to find my mom, and that's still what I plan to do."

"How?" Finn asked.

Julian rolled his eyes.

"On my mom's laptop," Eleanor said, "I found an email she wrote to your dad." She then told them what it read, including the coordinates, which could now be shared without revealing her Sync, and then she filled them in on her theory about what had happened.

"Makes perfect sense," Finn said when she finished.

"No, it doesn't," Julian said. "We need to give Skinner those coordinates. Right now."

"No," Eleanor said. "We can't risk that."

"I agree with her," Finn said.

"Are you kidding me?" Julian said. "This again?"

"The coordinates most likely point to the energy deposit," Eleanor said. "Let's say Skinner reaches it but our parents aren't there. What then? Skinner will have what he wants. You think he's going to keep looking for our parents?"

Julian snorted. "He wouldn't just give up like that."

"He might," Luke said. "Much as I hate to admit it." He pointed at Eleanor. "If this theory of yours is true, Skinner could easily say he put in a good-faith effort, cut his losses, and move on with whatever he finds out there. Wouldn't be the first time, from what I hear."

"He's the *CEO*, Julian," Finn said. "Think about it.

What's he even doing up here in the first place?"

Julian just shook his head, like he was trying not to let any words or thoughts in, but that only lasted a moment, after which he settled, leaned forward on his elbows, and blew into his fists. Eleanor could imagine the argument he was having with himself. He'd put all his hope for his dad's safe return in Skinner. And it was hard to let go of hope.

"I don't like what this means either," Eleanor said to him. "It means we're on our own."

"So what do we do?" Finn asked.

"We get to those coordinates," Eleanor said. "We see for ourselves what's there."

"In case you forgot"—Julian pointed at the wall—"there's a polar storm out there right now."

Eleanor hadn't forgotten. In fact, now that the cold had been given a taste of her, she could almost feel it prowling around the station, waiting for another opening to tear into her, and she feared it even more than before.

"We need to steal a transport," she said.

CHAPTER
15

"I'M JUST GONNA PRETEND I'M NOT HEARING ANY OF this," Luke said. "Honestly, kid. After what almost happened to you, you're—"

"Luke"—Eleanor spread her hands—"you *just* agreed that Skinner would stop the search for our parents."

"Yeah," Luke said, "I did, and he might. But that doesn't mean I think it's anything but suicide for someone to—"

"The station has three transports that I've seen," Finn said. "They keep them nearby."

"Hey," Luke said, "I'm not finished—"

"Can either of you drive one of those?" Eleanor asked.

Julian nodded. "My dad showed me once when we were in Canada. But that was a while ago."

"Hey," Luke said, a little louder. "Are you guys even listening to me?"

"Everyone will be awake soon," Eleanor said. "Maybe we should get back to our rooms for now. Pretend like everything is normal. I think Skinner already knows I lied about the password to the laptop. We don't need him suspecting us of anything else."

Julian and Finn nodded, then started to rise, but before they reached their feet, Luke slammed his fist down hard on the table, causing them to fall back into their seats.

"Stop talking and listen to me," he said. "What you are talking about doing is insane."

"No, Luke," Eleanor said. "It's *desperate*. Like us. So unless you're going to rat us out to Skinner, which I don't think you are, there isn't anything you can do to stop us." She folded her arms and looked directly into his eyes for several moments. "So are you?"

Luke glowered. "Am I what?"

Finn spoke up. "Are you going to rat us out?"

Luke narrowed his eyes. He glanced downward, in the direction of the tunnel, and actually seemed to be thinking about his answer. Eleanor hadn't even thought it would be a question.

"Luke . . ." She swallowed. "Please don't."

"Relax." Luke scratched his beard. "I'm not going to rat anyone out. Frankly, all I really want is for this storm to break so I can take off and get out of here."

"Great," Finn said. "So let us go."

"Or you could help us," Eleanor said.

Luke laughed. "*Help* you?"

"Yeah," she said. "Because I know you're a good guy."

Luke sucked air through one side of his teeth. "Here's the deal. I'm not gonna get in your way, but I'm also not gonna help you. There's only so much I'll have on my conscience when you three get yourselves killed. Understood?"

Eleanor didn't try to hide her disappointment and anger. "Understood."

"Good," he said. "Now if you don't mind, you all woke me up way too early. I'll see you in a few hours." He left them alone in the kitchen and stomped back down the spiral staircase toward the sleeping quarters.

The three of them waited until he was gone.

"He won't tell Skinner, will he?" Julian asked.

"No," Eleanor said. "He'll do exactly what he said he would."

"We don't need him," Finn said. "You have the coordinates, and Julian can drive a transport."

189

"Right." Eleanor inhaled and gave a sharp sigh. "So, now we just need a plan."

Later that morning, they met in the kitchen for breakfast, acting as though they had just woken up. Eleanor didn't know about Finn and Julian, but she hadn't gone back to sleep. She hadn't even tried, because she knew it wasn't going to happen. Luke was already sitting at a table, yawning over his coffee, and Dr. Marcus was there, too. She stood by as Eleanor and Finn made some instant oatmeal.

"Did you all sleep well?" Dr. Marcus looked at Eleanor. "It was your first night here at Polaris Station."

"I slept fine," Eleanor said.

Luke chortled at that.

"Something amusing, Mr. Fournier?" Dr. Marcus asked.

Eleanor tensed, while Luke took a sip of his coffee. "I'm more comfortable sleeping on my plane than inside this tin can."

Dr. Marcus pursed her lips. "You are welcome to return to your plane at any time." She then turned her attention back to Eleanor, Finn, and Julian. "I have some exciting news. The storm is expected to break tomorrow, and we have scheduled a plane to fly you home."

"No!" Eleanor shouted, almost reflexively, and everyone looked at her. "You can't do that."

"She's right," Finn said, more calmly. "We're not leaving."

"Children." The patronizing way Dr. Marcus inflected the word reminded Eleanor of the start to an old-fashioned bedtime story. "Were it not for the storm, you would already be gone. This is no place for you."

"But our parents . . . ," Julian said.

"We will continue the search," Dr. Marcus said. "But your presence here does not help with that. What it does do is put you at greater risk, which I am certain is the last thing your parents would want."

Eleanor shook her head. "But you can't—"

"This is not up for discussion," Dr. Marcus said. "I was merely informing you of what will happen." With a curt nod and a pivot on her toes, she marched away.

Eleanor swung a look at Julian and Finn. Then she glanced at Luke.

He shrugged. "That's what I would do if I were her."

"I wasn't asking," she said.

"Today is our one chance to search," Finn said. "If the storm breaks tomorrow like she said, we won't have another shot."

"So let's do this," Julian said.

They had made a simple plan before going back to bed. Polaris Station had a main entrance in the first pod, the one Eleanor had entered through, but each pod had its own emergency exits as well. Finn's job would be to disable the alarm on the emergency exit on their third pod. Julian would obtain one of the transport keys, which were kept near the main entrance in the first pod. During all of this, Eleanor would distract Skinner. Then they would all meet back up in their third pod, gather the gear they needed, leave through the emergency hatch, and head out onto the ice in the transport.

The three of them rose from the table and went to complete their assignments. Finn went down the staircase to the bottom level of the pod, where the escape hatch was located. Eleanor and Julian went toward the tunnel.

It was wide open now, but Eleanor still froze at the entrance.

Julian climbed in, then looked back. "You okay?"

Eleanor clenched her hands into fists at her side. "Yeah." Then she made herself climb in.

The door stayed open behind her this time, and the warmed air from the pods flowed through it, though Eleanor could still hear the storm outside, almost taunting her, reminding her in its ragged voice of how close it had come to claiming her.

They reached the far side and went to the command module. Skinner was there, and Eleanor approached him, her chin high.

"Could I try a few more passwords on my mom's computer?" she asked.

Skinner's eyebrows went up. "Certainly. I'd say this represents a change in attitude."

"Not really," Eleanor said. "Maybe you just have me all wrong."

"I would be pleased for that to be the case." Skinner went to the desk, reached into the drawer, and pulled out the laptop. "Take your time, Miss Perry."

Eleanor lifted the screen and started typing more fake passwords. She couldn't make it too obvious, but having seen what was on the laptop, and then deleted the one email she'd found, she felt like she could give Skinner something. Enough to distract him for a little while and allay his suspicions, anyway. She just had to hope that she hadn't missed anything important in her previous search of the computer. Julian stood nearby, waiting for his cue to leave.

A few minutes later, Eleanor exclaimed, "Got it!"

"You did?" Skinner leaned in, his voice rising in excitement. "What was it?"

"EllBell," Eleanor said. "It's a nickname my uncle Jack gave me."

"Charming." Skinner rotated the laptop toward him. "Well done, Miss Perry, well done." He immediately started opening files and typing searches, much the same way Eleanor had the previous night. In a matter of moments, it seemed Eleanor and Julian had faded from Skinner's awareness.

That was when Julian slipped away, without even looking in Eleanor's direction. She noticed him going but didn't look his way, either. She kept her focus on Skinner and the laptop. She was sure a tech guy could dump all the data and find the deleted email, but that would take a lot of time.

Skinner's eyes flicked back and forth across the screen, up and down, constantly moving.

"Do you think this will help find her?" Eleanor asked.

It took a moment for him to respond, and even then, his voice sounded absent. "Hmm, perhaps."

"What are you finding on there?" she asked.

"Nothing of relevance yet," he said.

Eleanor waited a few moments, watching a scowl form and deepen across his face. It seemed he was as frustrated as she had been. At one point, he looked up at her. "Is there something else you need?"

"Oh, uh, no." Eleanor gave him a sheepish shrug. "I—I'm just hoping you're going to find something."

He looked back at the screen. "Where did Mr. Powers go?"

Eleanor clamped down the sudden fear. Skinner may have noticed Julian's absence, but that didn't mean he truly suspected anything. "Oh," she said, trying to make it sound as if she had just noticed he was gone. "I don't know."

Skinner went back to skimming the laptop.

Eleanor waited, but shortly after that, her presence began to feel awkward, obvious, even to her. Skinner glanced up periodically and seemed to be growing increasingly irritated.

"I can come tell you if I find something," he finally said. "There is no need for you to hover."

"Sorry," Eleanor said. "I'm just . . . worried."

"Well . . . maybe you should go worry somewhere else," he said, without any hint of compassion or patience.

In the next moment, Julian was standing next to her, his chest rising and falling quickly, like he was trying to hide being out of breath. Eleanor and he avoided looking at each other, but Skinner's eyes shot up.

"Where have you been, Mr. Powers?" he asked.

"Just ran back to our pod to talk to my brother." Julian gestured to the laptop. "Did you find anything?" Julian asked.

"Not yet," Skinner said. "And one anxious child breathing over me is quite enough without adding a second. Why don't you both return to your pod, and should I find something worth noting, I will certainly inform you."

Eleanor and Julian nodded and left the command module. At the tunnel, Julian gave her a thumbs-up as he climbed in. He'd scored the key to a transport. Eleanor followed him, her excitement driving away some of her fear at the crossing.

Back in their pod, they waited in the kitchen until Finn appeared.

"Did you get the key?" he asked.

Julian nodded. "You get the alarm?"

Finn glanced over his shoulder at the staircase. "I think so. I cut the power line, and I didn't find an internal battery. I don't think it will go off."

"I guess that means we're ready," Eleanor said. But she couldn't leave without doing one last thing. "Give me just a minute?"

They nodded, and she left them and went down to the sleeping quarters. Then she walked up to Luke's room and knocked on the door. It whooshed open, and he propped an arm on the doorframe above his head, leaning toward her.

"What is it, kid?"

Eleanor took a breath. "Look. Even though you're not helping us now, I wanted to say thanks for all you've done for me. I couldn't have made it this far without you. I mean it. You saved my life. So . . . thank you."

Luke nodded. "Hope you find what you're looking for."

Eleanor nodded once more but didn't leave.

"Something else on your mind, kid?"

"I—I guess I was just thinking that after this is all over . . . when I'm back in Phoenix with my mom . . . maybe when you're in Phoenix . . ."

Luke's mustache twitched with a bit of grin. "You can come see *Consuelo* anytime."

Eleanor smiled and turned to leave.

"Hey, kid." Luke's voice softened. "I've been thinking about something you said when we first met. Anyone thinks you're a freak who doesn't fit needs to rearrange themselves."

Eleanor wanted to hug him for that, but resisted. "Thanks, Luke."

"You really doing this?"

"We are."

"I truly don't want to see you hurt."

"I won't get hurt." She turned away before he could try again to talk her out of their plan. She didn't want to argue with him after what they'd just said. "Bye, Luke."

"So long, kid."

A few moments later, she rejoined Finn and Julian, and the three of them went to their rooms and dressed in their polar gear. Eleanor moved the Sync from her pants pocket to a pocket in her coat. She grabbed her pack and headed for the pod's supply stores. They took a hermetic tent, food, lights, power packs, micro-generators, a GPS unit, anything they could fit that seemed useful. When they reached the point where they couldn't stuff any more in, they went to the emergency hatch and put on their masks.

Finn took hold of the hatch's handle. "Ready?" he said, his voice metallic.

"Let's hope you got the alarm," Julian said.

Finn took a breath, a hiss through his mask, and pulled. The hatch fell open. No alarm, but the storm blared inward at them. There was no staircase like there had been at the main entrance. They would have to drop to the snow below.

Julian leaped first. "Let's do this!"

Eleanor and Finn watched him fall, but the snow

was deep enough that he seemed to land easily. After he'd scrambled out of the way, Finn motioned for Eleanor to go next. She dropped her pack ahead of her and sat down on the ledge, dangling her feet over the opening, feeling the wind snatching at her boots as it circled below her like a pack of waiting wolves. It reminded her of a moment not too long ago, perched on a sled, high above a construction site at her school. Nothing and no one would stop her now.

She pushed off, eyes open, falling through the storm's teeth, right into its open maw.

— CHAPTER —
16

S HE LANDED HARDER THAN SHE'D THOUGHT SHE WOULD, but it didn't hurt. The force of the wind against her felt stronger than the force of gravity, blowing snow sideways at her. She rolled out from under the hatch so Finn could follow her, which he did a moment later.

Then the three of them labored to their feet in waist-high snow that had gathered around the hydraulic feet of the spheres. From the outside, the pods seemed larger than they had on the inside, and even larger than Eleanor remembered them.

"That way!" Julian pointed.

The transports sat half buried in a row several yards away. Eleanor, Finn, and Julian trudged toward them, the strain burning Eleanor's leg muscles within moments. Her mask had a hard time keeping up with her heavy breathing, letting a little bit of cold into her lungs.

But she told herself they would be out of the storm soon, when they reached the armored transports and got inside one of them. So far, everything had played out as they'd planned, and they were almost there.

As they drew closer, Finn asked, "Which one is ours?"

Julian held up the key and looked at it. "I think it's the middle one!"

They quickened their pace and reached the rear end of the vehicles a moment later.

"Hurry!" Eleanor said. "Let's—"

Two figures in polar gear stepped out from between the transports. One of them was Luke. The other—

"Miss Perry!" he shouted. "Mr. Powers and Mr. Powers!"

Skinner. Eleanor felt her legs wobbling under her from exhaustion and disbelief. Luke had sold them out.

"Turn around, all of you!" Skinner said. "March back to Polaris Station! Immediately!"

Eleanor didn't move. Neither did Finn and Julian. They would never have another chance to go searching for their parents. Eleanor's mom was out there, somewhere. She'd come so far, and gotten so close. The transport was right in front of them. But so was Skinner.

"NOW!" he shouted, his anger rivaling the storm.

"You lied!" Eleanor shouted at Luke.

"Better that than letting you die," Luke said. "I can live with a lie on my conscience."

Finn leaned in close. "What should we do?"

"I don't know," Julian said. "Think we can make it into the transport?"

"They'll just follow us," Eleanor said.

"If you do not move now," Skinner shouted, "I will have you brought back by force."

"Oh, yeah?" Julian shouted. "How're you going to do that?"

A third figure stepped out from between the other transports. Eleanor stopped breathing for a moment, choking on a gasp. A giant of a man strode toward them. Eleanor knew him. She knew the polar bear pelt he wore.

It was Boar.

"WHAT?" Luke shouted. "What is HE doing here?"

"He works for me," Skinner said.

Boar worked for Skinner? But he had tried to rob her. The giant had almost reached them, and Eleanor didn't know what to do.

Luke turned abruptly to Skinner. "The G.E.T. hires thieves?"

"Relax, Mr. Fournier," Skinner said. "Boar seized the initiative when he saw Miss Perry, perhaps a bit zealously. He knew I needed her Sync. But he is the best bounty hunter in Barrow."

The giant was only a couple of steps away now. "Told you this wasn't over, girl."

"Stay away from her!" Finn shouted.

He and Julian leaped in front of her, and both looked ready to fight what would clearly be a losing battle. But before either of them had the chance, Luke charged at Boar from behind, striking him in the lower back with his shoulder, the impact taking them both down.

"Run, kid!" Luke shouted, grappling with Boar on the ground. "I was wrong! Get out of here!"

The giant had almost regained his feet, in spite of Luke's efforts to keep him down.

"Stay where you are, Miss Perry!" Now Skinner charged toward them. "Don't move!"

Eleanor looked at Finn and Julian. Luke was right. They had to run. Eleanor didn't know what Skinner intended, but if he was willing to hire men like Boar, the situation was even worse than she had suspected.

She tried to bolt, but just then Boar lunged up and

got ahold of a strap on her pack, almost yanking her off her feet. She screamed, managed to wiggle out of the straps, and then ran.

A backward glance revealed Finn and Julian right behind her. Luke had Boar in a desperate grip around his waist, holding him back, while Skinner shouted something at them Eleanor couldn't hear over the storm. A few paces later, the whiteout erased them.

"Where are we going?" Julian shouted.

"I don't know!" Eleanor said. "Just keep running!"

Just keep running.

Eleanor had no idea how far they had gone. The storm made it impossible to measure the distance, but to her legs, it felt as though she had run miles. However, it turned out the endless expanse of the ice sheet did offer them one single advantage. Without anything to pile up against, the snow blew horizontally across the surface, scouring the ice without accumulating, so Eleanor didn't have to plow through deep snow anymore.

"I'm too tired!" Finn shouted. "I need to rest!"

"Me too!" Eleanor said.

The three of them collapsed together to the ground, huddling tightly, pressing their heads together in a circle, the wind and snow at their backs.

"Who *was* that other guy?" Finn asked, close enough that he no longer needed to shout.

"His name is Boar," Eleanor said. "He tried to rob me when I first got to Barrow."

The storm assaulted the silence that followed between them. There had been no time to really consider what Boar's presence back at the station really meant. No doubt remained in Eleanor's mind over Skinner's intentions. He had never been interested in finding Eleanor's mom, or even in Eleanor's safety. His sole purpose for being in the Arctic had been to find what Eleanor's mom had discovered, and he had been willing to lie and steal to obtain that information.

"What do we do now?" Julian asked.

"He got your pack," Finn said, looking over Eleanor's shoulder. That meant they had lost all their supplies. Their tent, their food, their power. Everything. They were stranded the same way her mother had been. "Without the GPS, we won't even know where we're going!"

But Eleanor had one last hope. She reached into her pocket, pulled out her Sync, and brought it to the center of their huddle.

"What's that?" Julian asked.

"This is what Skinner wanted," Eleanor said.

"You mean you had it all along?" Finn said.

Eleanor nodded.

"How did you know not to trust him?" Finn asked.

"My mom sent me a bunch of files before she disappeared and told me not to show anyone. I figured that included Skinner."

"And me and Finn, apparently," Julian said.

"May I remind you," Eleanor said, "not too long ago, *you* were threatening to go to Skinner."

Julian fell silent.

"But I'm trusting you both now," she said. "We can use the GPS on the Sync."

"To go where?" Julian asked.

"The coordinates," Eleanor said. "We can't go back. Our only option is to go forward."

"We don't have any supplies," Julian said. "We're not going to last long out here."

"We just have to last long enough to get to the coordinates," Eleanor said.

"What was in the files?" Finn asked.

Eleanor pulled them up to show him. It was the first time she had dared to look since her mom had sent them. With what Eleanor had learned, they seemed to make a little more sense. The network of lines crisscrossing the world map looked like they might be telluric currents. They intersected in concentrations at certain points, like Egypt and China, and Eleanor realized those sites were the same locations that nutty Dr. Johann von Albrecht had written about.

"Whoa," Finn said.

"What?" Eleanor asked.

"The energy measurements on those ley lines are off the charts." Then he pointed to a star map. "What's that?"

"I don't know why she had this," Eleanor said.

"Can I see it?"

Eleanor passed the Sync to him.

"Guys," Julian said, "we don't have time for this. Every second we waste—"

"This is weird," Finn said. "This isn't supposed to be here."

"What isn't?" Eleanor asked.

"Guys!" Julian shouted. "Seriously?"

Finn traced his fingers along the arcs and curves. "The distances between earth and the other planets are completely off. And there's an extra orbit."

"Extra?" Eleanor asked.

"According to this chart, there's something here that shouldn't exist."

"Something where?" Julian asked, suddenly interested.

Finn pointed upward. "Out *there*."

"Something like what?" Eleanor asked.

"I don't know, it doesn't say." Finn shook his head. "Just something . . . *big.*"

A sudden gust of wind ripped between them, shoving them into one another, and Finn almost fumbled the Sync. But he snatched it back before the storm could carry it away.

"Okay," Julian said. "Okay, that's enough. We need to move. They could be following us."

Eleanor and Finn agreed with him. Eleanor took the Sync back and pulled up the GPS. She plugged in the coordinates of the energy site and set their course.

"How far away is it?" Finn asked.

Eleanor stared at the screen, not wanting to think about the answer or say it out loud. "Thirty-two miles."

If Finn or Julian responded, the storm stole their replies. But they didn't need to say anything. If the answer had been five or ten miles, it would have seemed a difficult distance on the ice sheet without supplies. Thirty-two miles edged on impossible.

"How long will the power last in our suits?" Julian asked. The nanotech that gave them warmth ran on limited energy, like everything else.

"Not that long," Finn said. "But we can't go back, not now."

"Then we better get started," Julian said.

"At least the storm will cover our tracks," Eleanor said.

She put the Sync back in her pocket, and they set off in the direction of the site, pressing forward through the wind. As she walked, it lashed at her as if trying to strip her to the bone, with no intention of letting up, gleeful that it could finally reach her. But the wind was only one of the dangers they faced. Eleanor had read about crevasses, too. Fissures that opened up in the ice without warning, or hid under the snow, waiting to take you down, down, down to who knew where.

They trudged ahead for what felt like hours, pausing periodically to check the Sync and make sure they were on course. Without it, they would have been lost almost instantly. In the harsh and terrifying emptiness of the storm, there was no landmark, no horizon, no world beyond their short range of sight. Even with Finn and Julian at her side, Eleanor had never felt so cut off. From everyone and everything. They were alone at the top of the world, swallowed up, and she didn't know if they could escape the belly of this beast.

More time passed.

When next they paused to look at the Sync, Finn asked, "How far have we gone?"

Eleanor checked. Then rechecked. "Six miles," she said.

Storm silence followed.

"That's it?" Julian asked. "Only six?"

At this pace, the power in their suits would fail about three quarters of the way to the coordinates. The possibility of turning back crossed Eleanor's mind once again, and once again the image of Boar waiting there for her drove that thought away. Going forward was their only hope, as desperate as it seemed.

A few miles later, the air took a turn, growing sharper and colder. It was afternoon, and afternoon would soon lead to night. That thought shot a terror through Eleanor that set her hands shaking. They had no tent or shelter, and nothing could survive an Arctic night in the open.

Nothing but the shadows she'd seen. . . .

Even through her mask, she could feel it. Not even her polar gear could withstand the ice and snow of night. As she walked, her breathing went quickly from tolerable to uncomfortable to painful. She couldn't imagine how cold it would be if she removed the mask.

Her body felt hollow, empty of any will. Her weakened legs seemed to be working only by habit and forward momentum, each step getting shorter and shorter. A couple of times, they gave out on her, and Eleanor dropped hard. Each time, Finn and Julian helped her struggle back to her feet, and she kept going, helping them in turn when they fell.

With the setting of the invisible sun, the white of the world had turned the color of old weathered steel. Less than a mile later, Eleanor felt the nanotech in her suit give out, abandoning her. It took only a few steps for the cold to move in, and soon the pain of it, the frigid air in her lungs, forced her breathing into the shallows. Without the oxygen it needed, her body weakened further, and she grew light-headed. Her thoughts loosened at the edges. Her mind wandered haphazardly, but she kept her eyes fixed on the blankness ahead.

Then something moved to her right. Eleanor turned to look, but the shadowy figure was there and gone in an instant.

"Did you guys see that?" she asked.

They hadn't. Perhaps she had imagined it.

"My suit is dead," Finn said, wheezing.

"Mine died a little while ago," Julian said. "I can't feel my feet."

"That might be frostbite," Finn said. "Can you wiggle your toes?"

Julian stamped his feet and almost lost his balance. "Yeah. I think."

"Then you're okay for now," Finn said.

Eleanor pulled out the Sync. They'd been traveling for ten hours, and they were still nine miles from the coordinates. Nine miles without functioning suits.

"How close are we?" Finn asked.

"Not far," Eleanor said. "Three miles."

She didn't know why she lied, but when Finn's shoulders slumped even lower, she was glad she had.

Julian put his arm around his brother's shoulder. "Come on. One mile at a time. You can do it."

Eleanor kept silent and followed the brothers as the three of them resumed their trek. Somehow, they made it another mile. And another. But the cold had its barbed claws in her, and she knew it would win eventually.

At one point she looked up, and through a break in the clouds she saw a patch of stars against a black sky, like a flag waving in the storm. Dr. Marcus had been right. If they had stayed in the station, if they had done what they were told, what Luke had told them to do, they would have been flying home the next day. By tomorrow night, Eleanor would have been back with Uncle Jack.

You can do it, Ell Bell.

She heard his voice as though he were next to her and shook her head. Hallucinations were a sign of hypothermia. She closed her eyes.

A flag with stars. It was the Fourth of July. A sunny day. Warm enough in Phoenix for a 5K that year.

You can do it, and I'll be right there beside you the whole way.

Eleanor looked down the road. The icy endless road.

You can do it, Ell Bell.

Will you stay with me?

Of course. You lead the way.

Eleanor pushed herself. She'd never run so fast, or so far, the road not as endless as she feared, and when she crossed the finish line, she and Uncle Jack walked to the edge of that road and threw themselves down on their backs, side by side in the snow.

Eleanor looked up at the smothering sky, and a howling wind in her ear dragged her partway back to the ice sheet. Finn lay on the ground next to her, Julian kneeling over him, shaking him by the shoulders. Eleanor didn't understand. Where was Uncle Jack? They had crossed the finish line together. She thought they had made it.

She pulled out her Sync, checked the GPS. They *had* made it. They were only a few hundred feet from the coordinates. But this couldn't be it. There was nothing here. Nothing but barren ice. Nothing but storm and gray and cold. They had risked their lives and made it here for all this *nothing*.

That was when the Sync lit up and chimed. A familiar sound. A glorious sound that cut through raging wind.

There was a message from her mom.

— CHAPTER —
17

E LEANOR PULLED THE SCREEN CLOSE.

        <Eleanor, where are you?> the message read.

Eleanor smiled, a movement that hurt the frozen muscles in her cheeks. She tried to type a response.

    <I here>

    <Where?>

    <Rit here ucant see me?>

    <I can't see you, Eleanor. I'm not with you. Where are you?>

    <finish line uncl jack>

    . . .

    <mom>

    <Pay attention to me, Eleanor. You need to focus. I need

you to tell me where you are.>

Eleanor forced her mind together, gathering up all the loose fragments and fuzz. She had to answer her mother, but she didn't know how. So she typed the numbers she had memorized, the coordinates, as accurately as she could.

<70 56 28 24 156 53 27 80>

. . .

<mom those are cordinates remmbr>

<Yes, Eleanor. We are on our way.>

<u coming?>

. . .

<mom>

. . .

<mom>

. . .

<love you>

. . .

Eleanor put the Sync back in her pocket and turned her head toward Julian and Finn. Both now lay in the snow.

"My mom is coming," she said, her voice sounding odd inside her head. Had she said it out loud? What was wrong with her? The cold could make you stupid, she knew that, but Eleanor didn't feel cold. Maybe she was tired. Maybe she just needed to sleep and wake up and then everything would make sense. She closed her eyes.

Shadows moved.

Paws. Fur. Teeth.

A voice. Sounds not words. Words not words.

Her bed fell away, the ground where she wanted to sleep.

Put me back.

She felt something. Something she had forgotten. Warmth. More fur.

Another shadow, this one tall, more words not words.

She was moving.

A familiar voice woke her. "Eleanor."

She opened her eyes. Finn leaned over her, gently shaking her. Julian sat next to him. They were in some kind of hut built out of massive, bleached-white bones and a covering of animal hide. It smelled of woodsmoke, leather, and the dirt floor beneath them.

Eleanor sat up, covered in furs. "Where are we?"

"Don't know." Julian rubbed his head. "Just woke up."

Eleanor dredged her mind for what memories she could find in the murk of their trek across the ice. She

217

knew they had somehow made it to the coordinates, or close to them, but there wasn't anything there. And she remembered Uncle Jack for some reason. That had to be some kind of hallucination, which meant hypothermia.

Finn looked around. "This hut is . . . Paleolithic. I mean, look at these bones."

Some were as thick as Eleanor's waist, stubby, like leg bones. Ribs as tall as Finn arched overhead from a foundation of vertebrae. They were basically sitting inside the rearranged skeleton of something huge.

"I think they're from a woolly mammoth," Finn said.

Eleanor's head had started throbbing, and pain flared in her joints as she moved. Pockets of memory continued to bubble up. Images Eleanor didn't trust. "Hey," she said, "do you guys remember . . . wolves?"

Julian shook his head, while Finn's gaze went vacant. A moment later, he said, "Actually, I think I do."

So they shared that, at least. Then Eleanor remembered trying to type something. She threw the furs off and dug frantically into her pocket.

"What is it?" Finn asked.

"My mom!" She pulled up the Sync, staring at a string of new messages, some of which Eleanor had typed that made no sense. "Look," she whispered, and showed them the screen.

"Is that how we got here?" Julian asked. "Did they find us?"

Eleanor struggled to her feet, each bend and flex of her body an ordeal. She had to see what was outside the hut. She hobbled toward the entrance, an arched opening framed by what looked like mammoth tusks, pushed aside a flap of animal hide, and stepped through.

She gasped at what she saw.

An enormous ice cavern opened wide before her, its walls vast enough to hold several city blocks, its ceiling high enough for a bird to soar. Columns of light crossed the vaulted space at intersecting angles, and where they landed, grass grew. The air felt cool, but not cold, like a summer day back in Phoenix, and the ground rose in gentle hills and dipped in shallow washes, studded here and there with large, pale boulders.

Several other bone huts surrounded her. And people. They wore clothing made mostly of furs and skins, with a few roughly woven fabrics. There were men and women, some working outside the doorways to their huts, others standing around a large fire pit. They all had dark-brown or black hair, with deeply tanned skin, and prominent brows jutting over deep-set eyes.

Their eyes.

Black voids as endless as the ice sheet, somehow not right, not human, and all of them had turned to stare at her. Eleanor had never felt less like she belonged in a place.

Finn and Julian came out of the hut behind her, and both of them went rigid.

"You," one of the men said, his voice guttural. He strode toward them with an energy Eleanor could somehow sense, but not identify. Like she was looking at him through heat vision goggles. "You wait," he said, and motioned for them to go back into the hut. Not angrily. But firmly.

"Wait for what?" Julian whispered.

Finn backed away. "I don't know, but I think we better do what he says."

They reentered the hut, sat down, and just looked at one another in stunned silence. Eleanor imagined her expression matched the wide-eyed, exhausted disbelief she saw on Finn and Julian.

"I feel like I must still be hallucinating," Eleanor finally said.

"Can two people have the same hallucination?" Finn asked. "Because I'm having it, too."

Except Eleanor knew that wasn't true. This was all

real, this hut, this village, this cave, and there had to be an explanation for it, even if she couldn't imagine what it might be. "Okay," she said. "Let's think about this logically. What's the last thing you remember?"

For all of them, it was the storm. Collapsing in the snow. And for Eleanor and Finn, there were wolves.

"Have either of you heard rumors of people seeing wolves out on the ice?" Eleanor paused. "Or . . . an Inupiat hunter?"

Julian and Finn both nodded, and Finn said, "I overheard one of the scientists saying he'd seen something like that. Everyone laughed at him."

"Back in Barrow," Eleanor said, "this guy, a mechanic, said there was *something* going on out here. I think we've solved that mystery."

"Maybe," Finn said, then pointed at the hut's entrance. "But I don't think those people out there are Inupiat."

Eleanor had to agree with him. This village and its inhabitants felt utterly removed from the world. Almost alien. And with each moment that passed in this place, she became more aware of a deep . . . sensation. A kind of hum she felt but couldn't quite hear. These people, the bones of this hut, even the ground beneath them, all seemed to resonate with it.

"Can you guys feel that?" she asked.

"Feel what?" Julian said.

Finn turned his head at an angle, like he was trying to listen for something, and then shrugged.

"*That*. It's like we're in the middle of a big machine or something." Eleanor looked from Finn to Julian; both of them looked back at her with the same expression Jenna used when she called Eleanor a freak. "Nothing. Never mind."

"Okay," Julian said. "So. If they're not Inupiat, who are they? How did they get here?"

"Where is here?" Finn said. "From the glance I got outside, I think we're under the ice sheet, but—"

"We'd have to be." Julian thumped his boot. "We're down to solid ground. That means we're miles from the surface of the glacier."

"How is that possible?" Eleanor said. "We—"

The hide flap over the entrance whipped open, and she turned toward the figure who entered. A mere second of disbelief carried Eleanor into the next moment, when everything changed.

"Mom?"

Shock, joy, relief—each filled a second of its own. "Mom!" Eleanor leaped to her feet and dove into her mother's arms.

"Eleanor?" her mother said, squeezing her tight. "My God, Eleanor!"

"Mom," Eleanor whispered, and felt her mother trembling. This was real. This was all real. Somehow, Eleanor had succeeded. She had come here, into the farthest reaches, and found her mother alive.

At that thought, Eleanor's chest heaved, halfway between laughter and crying, and big fat tears wet her cheeks. She had never given voice to the fear that her mom was dead, but she had been carrying it with her all this time, and now she could let it go.

"I love you, Mom," Eleanor said.

"I love you, too." Her mother squeezed her again. "I still can't believe—sweetie, you're here. You're *here*."

Eleanor pulled away enough to look into her mother's face, her cheeks and forehead peeling from sunburn and windburn, her eyes brimming with her own tears. "I came to find you," Eleanor said.

Her mother covered her mouth and shook her head. "I can't believe it."

"Dr. Perry?" Julian said.

Eleanor had forgotten that he and Finn were there.

"Oh my goodness," her mom said. "Julian! Finn!"

"Do you know where our dad is?" Finn asked.

"Yes!" her mother said. "Yes, he was right behind me. He's probably just outside."

The two brothers looked at each other. Then they

ran from the hut, and Eleanor heard them calling for their father.

Her mother put her arm over Eleanor's shoulder. "I'd like to see this," she said, and guided Eleanor from the hut in time to watch Dr. Powers gather his sons, one in each arm, into the same tight hug. Dr. Powers was a broad-shouldered man, with a darker complexion than Julian and Finn, and narrow, glinting eyes that made him look permanently curious.

The villagers stood around them watching, whispering to one another, and smiling. One of them, the tallest in the village who Eleanor could see, stood apart. He had faint tattoos on his neck and held a long spear.

Dr. Powers kissed the tops of his boys' heads, then looked up at Eleanor's mother with an openmouthed grin. "Can you believe this, Sam?"

Sam? The only man Eleanor had ever heard call her mother Sam was Uncle Jack.

Her mother shook her head, laughing. "No, I truly can't."

Dr. Powers walked Julian and Finn toward Eleanor and her mom, an arm slung over the shoulders of each son. "I think we need to hear all about it," he said, and led them back into the hut.

Eleanor and her mother followed, and as they all

settled down on the ground in a circle, the tall villager Eleanor had noticed ducked inside. He carried a wide flat basket with him, which he set on the ground in the middle of the room, and then took a seat along the wall of the hut, bowing his head a little toward Julian and Finn, then Eleanor.

"This is Amarok," her mother said. "At least, that's what I call him. That's not his real name, which I still can't pronounce, but Amarok sounds close."

"He is the leader of the village," Dr. Powers said. "He's the one who spotted you on the ice and brought you down here."

Amarok bowed his head again. "Welcome," he said, his voice hard and smooth as a polished stone. He made a sweeping gesture with his hand around the hut. "Your home."

Eleanor thanked him, and so did Finn and Julian. The basket bore meat from some kind of small animal Eleanor couldn't quite identify, as well as a few berries.

Dr. Powers passed them a canteen. "You must be hungry and thirsty."

Eleanor was, and so were Finn and Julian, based on the way they tore into the food.

Eleanor's mother spoke while Eleanor and the others ate. "We've been teaching Amarok English."

"Who *is* he?" Eleanor took a drink and tipped her head toward the entrance. "Who are they?"

"In due time," her mother said. "First, I want to hear about you."

So after Eleanor had eaten, she told her mother about her journey to the Arctic, how she had stowed away on Luke's plane, then the events in Barrow, and the journey to Polaris Station. Then she told her about Skinner, and Boar, and the escape across the ice. Through that last part of the story, her mother and Dr. Powers kept exchanging looks with each other, Dr. Powers clenching his jaw, his neck tense.

After Eleanor told them about the last thing she remembered, passing out on the ice, he said, "We should have stopped Skinner when we had the chance."

"Not now, Simon," her mother said. "The data is safe—there's nothing he can do." She looked at Eleanor. "You did receive the files I sent, didn't you?"

"Yes," Eleanor said. "And I kept them secret, even though they kept trying to take my Sync."

"That's my girl," her mother said. "You don't have it with you, do you?"

Eleanor pulled it out of her pocket with a smile and handed it to her mother.

"Skinner wanted that stuff *bad*," Julian said.

"He wants this place," her mother said. "He wants the Concentrator."

"Concentrator?" Finn asked.

"That's what we call it," Dr. Powers said. "But that's only based on our theory that . . . You know what? Maybe it'd be better if we just showed you."

Their parents rose from the ground and led the way back out of the tent. Amarok followed behind them. They strolled through the village, and Eleanor smiled and nodded at the people she passed.

As they walked, her mother talked. "Some time ago, I detected an energy signature under the ice. It was relatively weak, nothing that I thought would be of any interest to Sohn International. But it was unlike anything I'd ever encountered, so out of curiosity I kept an eye on it."

They passed a dozen or so of the mammoth-bone houses before they reached the edge of the village, and then kept going. The ground turned a bit soggy and mossy, dotted by the occasional white microblossom. This was like the tundra that covered Missouri and Kansas.

"A little over a year ago," her mother said, "the signature changed. It grew stronger, more intense."

"That was when she finally got in touch with me

about it," Dr. Powers said, "since we both worked for Sohn. And together, we figured out what it was."

"Telluric energy?" Finn asked.

"Why, yes." Dr. Powers cocked his head at his son, seeming surprised. "How did—?"

"We figured out what Skinner was searching for," Finn said.

As they walked across the tundra, up and down with the rising ground and past the granite boulders, the humming sensation Eleanor had felt earlier grew louder in her mind. It filled the cavern. But no one else seemed aware of it, and she remembered the looks Julian and Finn had given her. *Freak.* She said nothing.

"Skinner." Eleanor's mother said the name with a hatred Eleanor had never heard in her before. "I went to the G.E.T. for help. But Skinner used his resources and power to take over our whole operation."

"Right before he arrived, we discovered this place." Dr. Powers looked around at the cavern as they started up a small hill.

"How?" Julian asked.

"We followed Amarok," her mother said. "We'd been hearing about sightings of a sled team on the ice. They were nothing but rumors, really, because how could anything survive out there? But one night, we were up on the surface studying the energy anomaly,

228

and Amarok just appeared from nowhere, as if he rose from the ground. That led us to the fissure in the ice, which we followed down here."

"And that's how we found *this*," Dr. Powers said.

They crested the hill. Below them, at the center of a wide crater, a black structure rose from the tundra. It was the size of Luke's plane, standing upright, a dark and twisted, metallic-looking tree that seemed to shift and slide, like a shadow within a shadow. Branches of varying lengths and thicknesses bent at odd angles around a central trunk, forming a brambled maze that defied Eleanor's attempts to make sense of it. At the sight of it, the humming in her head became almost deafening.

"What *is* that?" Julian asked.

"This is the Concentrator," Eleanor's mother said.

That didn't exactly answer Julian's question. But then, Eleanor couldn't have come up with a single word to describe the thing below her. She could barely settle on a definite shape. Its angles weren't square, or round, or sharp, or smooth. Its black surface seemed to shift and deflect her sight, denying its own existence.

"Why is it . . . ?" Finn started. "Why is it hard to see?"

Dr. Powers cleared his throat. "It seems to have physical and spatial properties we don't have the anatomical or cognitive ability to perceive."

"What?" Julian asked.

But Eleanor thought she knew what he meant. "It's like infrared light, right?" she said. "Our eyes can't see heat without special goggles, even though it's there."

"Exactly," Dr. Powers said. "Our naked eyes don't have infrared vision because we haven't needed it to survive. We didn't evolve that way."

Eleanor's mother grinned at her. "Devilishly clever."

"So it just grew here?" Julian asked.

"It doesn't seem to be a naturally occurring object," Dr. Powers said.

"Wait," Finn said. "You mean someone built it?"

"That's right," Dr. Powers said.

Finn continued, "And whoever made it had . . . different eyes?"

Eleanor's mother and Dr. Powers looked at each other. Then Dr. Powers said, "Different technology, at the very least."

Different eyes, different minds. Eleanor shuddered when she thought about what would make seeing that thing necessary to survive.

"WE CALL IT THE CONCENTRATOR BECAUSE WE *think* it's concentrating telluric current," her mother said. "This is the source of the signature we detected from the surface. Its energy is the reason Skinner took over our research, but from the beginning, Simon and I believed it would be very dangerous to harness the power here until we understood it. Which government put it here? Why? Skinner wouldn't listen, and he was about to fire us and force us from the station. So Simon and I took all our research and went out onto the ice. I sent my files to you, including the coordinates, and then I erased everything from my Sync. I didn't know what else to do to keep it from falling into Skinner's hands."

Her mother had pulled out an instrument, a kind of gun. It had a bundle of barrels above a grip, with a small computer screen and control panel at the back end.

"What's that?" Eleanor asked.

"A telluric scanner." Her mom switched the device on. "Without the calculations on my Sync, I haven't been able to calibrate it. We haven't had the ability to really study the Concentrator at all. I can't tell you how frustrating it has been. But now that you brought me this"—she held up Eleanor's Sync—"I can get back to work."

She manipulated the controls of the scanner, the computer screen wavering with oscillating curves. They descended toward the Concentrator, and Eleanor's mother paced around it, watching the readout, but as she did so, Eleanor felt a subtle shift in the humming around her, a change in tone.

"Simon, this is incredible," her mother said. "We were right. The concentration of telluric current here is . . ."

Dr. Powers stepped toward her. "Vectors?"

The humming smothered her mother's reply as she and Dr. Powers huddled together over the scanner.

Eleanor blinked and shook her head, averting her eyes from the Concentrator. The humming seemed to emanate from it, and it was getting worse. Something was happening, and it had begun when Eleanor's mother turned on the scanner.

"Look for subcurrents," Dr. Powers said.

"Right," her mother said. "Let me dial up the gain."

The humming swelled to a pounding rush, building, building, as if to something explosive. Eleanor wanted to cover her ears.

"Sweetie?" Her mother was looking at her. "Are you okay? You look flushed."

"I'm, uh . . ." The Concentrator seemed to be reaching out toward her, clawing at her mind. The humming felt so deafening she couldn't concentrate. "Could we—" Eleanor rubbed her temples. "Can we get away from here? Back to the village?"

"Of course, sweetie." Eleanor's mother turned to Dr. Powers. "Do you want to continue without me?"

"No, you need to be here for this." Dr. Powers looked at Eleanor, seeming worried. "Let's all head back. We shouldn't push them after their ordeal. It's probably exhaustion or dehydration."

Her mom switched off the scanner, and the humming immediately diminished. Eleanor sighed.

"Come, sweetie." Her mom put her arm around

Eleanor and shepherded her away from the black device. With each step they took out of the crater and across the tundra, the humming grew quieter still, and before long Eleanor felt herself returning to normal.

They had almost reached the edge of the village when something lumbered out ahead of them from behind one of the boulders. Something massive, and hairy, with long, curved tusks.

Julian yelped. "What the—!"

"Holy crap," Finn whispered. "That's . . . that's a woolly mammoth!"

The creature emitted a low, rumbling sound as it walked toward them. Its head and shoulders towered at least ten feet high, and the sharp smell of its hair and musk reached them well ahead of the animal, rousing Eleanor from the last aftereffects of the humming.

"She's tame," her mother said, pulling Eleanor close. "Just be still and watch."

She?

The mammoth's advance was quick and almost stumbling, the long cords of her brown coat swinging. When she reached Eleanor and the others, she stopped, huffing, the tips of her tusks but a couple of feet away, her eyes taking them in.

"Amarok's people have a name for her," her mother said. "Kixi."

"Odd," Dr. Powers said. "She seems a little agitated by something."

Eleanor did not like the idea of an agitated mammoth and wondered if Kixi could perhaps feel the humming, too. Weren't animals supposed to have the ability to sense earthquakes or something? Maybe it was like that. The mammoth lifted her trunk and extended it toward them, sniffing. Eleanor flinched a little as it drew near to her.

"Hold still," her mother whispered.

The tip of the trunk, which almost resembled a lip, touched Eleanor's forehead, gently, like the brush of a velvet curtain warmed by the sun coming in. Eleanor smiled as Kixi then blew a puff of air in her face, tossing her hair, before moving on with her heavy gait.

"She's heading out to graze," Dr. Powers said. "Magnificent creature."

In the mammoth's wake, Eleanor stood immobilized. So did Finn and Julian.

Dr. Powers chuckled at them. "All right, back to the hut. It's time to put all the pieces together."

Eleanor sat on the floor in the building made of mammoth bones, touching her forehead where Kixi had brushed it. She'd thought these bones were prehistoric, but now . . .

"Is it some kind of clone?" Finn asked.

"No," Eleanor's mother said.

"But . . ." Eleanor's mouth hung open. "How?"

"Exactly," Dr. Powers said. "That is exactly how we felt when we first saw this place. I'm not sure we've figured it all out yet, but I think we're close."

"As near as we can tell," her mother said, "Amarok and his people are from the late Pleistocene, in geological terms, or the Upper Paleolithic, in archaeological terms. From a period known as the Younger Dryas."

"The Stone Age?" Finn asked.

"Exactly," Eleanor's mother said. "Roughly twelve thousand years ago."

If Eleanor hadn't just been nuzzled by a woolly mammoth, she might have taken what her mother was saying as a sign of mental illness. But now she just sat and listened.

"The Younger Dryas was a period of rapid cooling," Dr. Powers said. "An ice age. Geologists still don't really know what caused it, because the Milankovitch cycles wouldn't have predicted it."

Eleanor noticed that he left the name *Skinner* off the cycles.

"It seems," Dr. Powers went on, "that Amarok and his people died in a catastrophe of some kind. A flood. A storm. We don't know, but something wiped them out with one shot, along with Kixi. Their whole village got buried in the permafrost, along with the Concentrator."

An unexpected, unpredictable ice age had destroyed Amarok's village and his people. Much the way another unexpected, unpredictable ice age was currently destroying Eleanor's.

"That is how it stayed for thousands of years," her mother said. "Until a few years ago, when the Concentrator began emitting energy. We believe the energy carved out this cave and somehow revived Amarok and his people. It's telluric. It's the earth's own life force. Believe me, as a rational empiricist, I know how incredible this sounds, and I have wrestled with these conclusions in spite of the evidence before my own eyes."

"Within the last year," Dr. Powers said, "its output has increased to the strength of a nuclear power plant, and it shows no signs of slowing down. In fact, it continues to increase."

"But who put it there?" Julian asked. "Where is the energy going?"

Dr. Powers turned to his son. "We don't know yet. But now that we have the Sync, we'll hopefully be able to answer those questions."

"But if the earth is losing energy from it," Finn

said, "is that thing causing the Freeze?"

Dr. Powers slowly rubbed his hands together. "We don't know, son. We simply don't know. But for now, I think you all need some more rest."

They spent the rest of that day avoiding any talk of the Concentrator, or even the woolly mammoth walking around. Finn and Julian went off with their dad, while Eleanor and her mom walked around the village, reunited against impossible odds.

"I missed you," her mother said. "After Simon and I came down here, I wondered if I'd ever see you again."

"When they told me you were lost," Eleanor said, "I wondered the same thing."

"I hate to ask this, but does Uncle Jack know where you are?"

"Not really." Eleanor worried about what Skinner might have told him after she ran away with Julian and Finn. "He knows I made it to the station, at least."

Her mom winced. "Poor Jack."

"In my defense, he had to expect this from me."

Her mom nodded. "You two seem to have an understanding of each other."

"Yeah."

"There are times I envy that."

"Mom . . . ," Eleanor said, but didn't know what to

follow it up with, because her mom had touched on something true. There were times Eleanor wished she had that kind of understanding with her mom, too.

"It's okay, sweetie," her mom said. "I get to love that you constantly surprise me. Like how you found your way here."

Eleanor felt a warmth blossom in her chest that no polar storm could drive out. "That's a nice way to look at it."

Her mom winked. "Better than blaming the Donor."

Eleanor laughed, and a few comfortably silent moments later, Amarok approached them. Eleanor sensed the same charge coming off him as the first villager, the one who had told them to wait in the hut. In fact, that force seemed to radiate from all the people in the village.

"You eat with us?" Amarok said.

Eleanor's mother bowed her head. "Yes. Thank you."

Amarok nodded and walked away. Eleanor watched him go, trying to imagine what it would be like to wake up to a world ten thousand years removed from hers, and couldn't. She wasn't even sure she could wrap her head around that long a time. "What will happen to them?" she asked.

Her mother sighed and shook her head. "I have

no idea. But I pity them. They're an unintentional by-product of something completely beyond their understanding. In a different time, before the Freeze, anthropologists would have wanted to study them."

"I wish they could hide down here forever."

"Hiding doesn't seem to be in Amarok's DNA. Simon and I—"

"Simon?"

Her mom blushed a little and looked at her feet. "Dr. Powers and I warned Amarok not to go up on the surface anymore. But he won't listen. He's even been to Barrow with his team of wolves."

"Really? I bet that freaked him out."

"Don't be so sure. They are *Homo sapiens*. As human as you and me. And one thing humans are good at is adapting." She waved Eleanor to her side. "Come on. Let's go eat."

"What's for dinner?" Eleanor asked.

"Rabbit, probably. The tundra down here is teeming with them."

They walked back through the village and joined with everyone around the communal fire pit. Finn and Julian were there with their dad, trying to talk to some of Amarok's people. The firelight felt warm against Eleanor's face, and the woodsmoke smelled spicy and deep. She took a seat next to her mother, ate stringy, charred meat with her fingers, and just watched.

Later, she listened as Amarok spoke to his people in his language. Eleanor recognized the sound of it from her snippets of memory of the previous night. He seemed to be telling a story, and with great flair. He moved around the fire, singing, almost dancing, adopting the postures of animals, conveying exaggerated emotion. His audience laughed, and it felt to Eleanor like any gathering of family and friends.

Her mom was right. They were like her, and she was like them, as much as she felt like anyone. Her awareness of this gave her hope. An ice age had claimed Amarok's people. Yet here they were, living, laughing, telling the stories they'd always told. Perhaps that meant there were things the ice couldn't contain. Perhaps its grip wouldn't last forever. Even in the face of a rogue world, even with the threat of insatiable ice, Amarok had his voice.

He came to sit by Eleanor later that evening. "Food good?"

Eleanor smiled and nodded. "It was very good. Thank you."

"Welcome," he said. Then he pointed his chin toward the edge of the village in the direction of the Concentrator. "You see *tawkeeshick?*"

"Yes," Eleanor said. Then she enunciated each

syllable of the next word. "Con-cen-tra-tor?"

"Yes, Concentrator," Amarok said. "*Tawkeeshick.*" He said the word with a seeming reverence.

So his people had a word for it—

Wait.

His demeanor when talking about the Concentrator, and the fact that his people had a word for it, caused Eleanor to wonder something else. She considered how to ask her next question. "Amarok, how long has *tawkeeshick* been here?"

Amarok frowned, clearly not understanding. The English he had learned was apparently still very limited.

Eleanor tried to simplify it. "When . . . *tawkeeshick?*"

"When?" Amarok asked. "*Tawkeeshick?*"

Eleanor nodded.

Amarok still frowned, but he looked skyward. "*Tawkeeshick . . .* before."

"Before? Before what?"

Amarok spread his arms wide. "Before village."

Did that mean what she thought it meant? "*Tawkeeshick* was here before your village?"

Amarok nodded. "*Tawkeeshick* here before."

But that would mean the Concentrator had been there for over twelve thousand years. That meant no modern government or company had put it there. But how was that possible?

Later that night, back in their mammoth-bone hut, Eleanor posed that question to her mother and the others. They were similarly bewildered.

"I don't understand," her mother said. "I knew they had a word for it. I guess I just assumed they invented it when the Concentrator revived them. Are you sure you understood him? Or that he understood you?"

"Very sure," Eleanor said.

A chilled silence lingered in the hut.

"I'm more certain of one thing," Dr. Powers said. "*No one* can get their hands on the Concentrator. Not until we know more, and right now it feels like we know less than when we started."

"But wait," Julian said. "Someone had to make that thing, right? I mean, it's not like it's natural."

Everyone agreed with him.

"But there's no way these cavemen made it," Julian continued.

Again, everyone agreed.

"Aliens made it," Finn said. "It's either that or the Concentrator is from the future. Right?"

"Pardon me," Eleanor's mother said, "but I am not prepared to go down either of those roads. It is far more likely we're dealing with an error in translation."

But Eleanor didn't believe there had been any error.

Dr. Powers cleared his throat. "Let's put this aside until we've had a good night's sleep. We'll look at it with fresh eyes in the morning."

They all went to bed a short time later, but Eleanor didn't fall asleep right away. She lay awake, thinking about what Finn had said.

Different eyes. Different minds.

What if he was right? Only a week ago, Eleanor would have laughed at the idea, but now, having come to this alien, Arctic place, and having seen and felt the Concentrator for herself, it didn't seem absurd at all.

When Eleanor finally did fall asleep, the black and terrible branches of the Concentrator twisted through her dreams.

— CHAPTER —
19

ELEANOR DIDN'T WANT TO RETURN TO THE CONCENTRA-
tor. But her mother refused to leave her alone in
the village, and Eleanor didn't feel like protesting. So
she braced herself against the hum as they crossed the
tundra once again. When they reached the crater, the
black tree rose up from the center as inscrutably as it
had the day before.

"See?" Finn said. "That looks alien to me."

"Son," Dr. Powers said, shaking his head.

But even in the light of a new day, Eleanor still
agreed with him, in spite of her mother's argument
for common sense. Eleanor knew what Amarok had
meant.

They descended into the crater, toward the Concentrator. The ever-present humming hadn't yet begun to assault Eleanor. She expected it to pummel her as soon as her mom turned the scanner on, but her mother didn't. Instead, she pulled out another, smaller instrument, along with Eleanor's Sync.

"Now," she said. "Let's figure out where the energy is going."

She and Dr. Powers both held up devices, walking around, measuring, conferring with each other. They worked, time passed, and Eleanor found herself growing somewhat accustomed to the strangeness of this place. The wrongness of the Concentrator never quite faded, but Eleanor found she could ignore it. Finn and Julian just seemed bored.

"You don't really think it's aliens, do you, bro?" Julian had his mouth cocked in a mocking grin.

Finn shrugged. "What's it to you?"

"I'm just embarrassed for you."

"Are you embarrassed for me, too?" Eleanor asked.

"Why?" Julian asked. "Don't tell me you believe it."

Eleanor also shrugged.

Sometime later, her mother and Dr. Powers walked over to them.

"It's not just a Concentrator," her mother announced. "It's also converting the telluric energy."

"Converting it into what?" Eleanor asked.

"Some form of energy we can't detect," her mother said. "But the telluric currents are definitely concentrating here, and the law of conservation says the energy must still exist in one form or another."

"What about dark energy?" Dr. Powers said.

"Simon." Eleanor recognized the condescending angle of her mother's gaze. "That is as improbable as—"

"Hear me out, Sam." Dr. Powers pointed up into the Concentrator's branches. "There is way too much energy pouring into this thing for us to lose all sign of it. Unless it's getting converted into something our instruments can't read."

"True," her mother said, stretching the word out.

"There aren't that many types of energy our instruments can't read," he said.

Eleanor thought back to science class. Theoretically, dark energy permeated the universe, more plentiful than any other kind of matter, but undetectable, as if outside our perception and existence. What if some-one—*something*—had figured out how to harness it?

"Dark energy would explain a lot," Dr. Powers said.

"But it doesn't explain where the energy is *going*," her mother said. "What, you think this dark energy is just shooting up into the vacuum of space?"

That sparked something in Eleanor's memory. All

this talk of aliens, and dark energy, and space—it all came together into something that haunted the edge of her thoughts.

"I don't know, Sam," Dr. Powers said. "But none of the likely scenarios have panned out. We're off the map here."

Map. Space.

"The star chart," Eleanor said.

Her mother turned to her. "What's that, sweetie?"

"You sent me a G.E.T. star chart." Eleanor pointed at the Sync in her mother's hand. "Finn said there was an extra orbit."

"That's right," Finn said.

Dr. Powers looked at Eleanor's mother.

"I never had a chance to look at some of the G.E.T. files I copied." Her mother brought up the Sync. "I suppose it might . . . Here it is." Then she and Dr. Powers began scanning the screen, staring at it for several moments. They looked up at each other.

"Simon," her mom said. "This can't be . . ."

"Finn, you were right," Dr. Powers said. "But it's not just an extra orbit. According to this, there's an extra planet in our solar system."

"What?" Julian said. "Did you just say an extra *planet?*"

Dr. Powers lowered his voice, almost to a whisper.

248

"Sam . . ." He shook his head. "This is—"

"This chart must be hypothetical," her mother said. "A simulation. It's just too—"

"I don't think it is," Dr. Powers said. "It explains everything."

"What does?" Finn asked.

Dr. Powers looked upward. "A rogue planet."

"Wait, what's a rogue planet?" Julian asked, sounding frustrated.

"They roam between solar systems," Dr. Powers said. "They start out orbiting a star, like any other planet, and then something happens. Their star goes supernova, they get knocked out of orbit by an asteroid, something like that, and they end up orphaned in space. Sometimes, they wander into another solar system, and their gravity plays havoc."

"That's why we're in an ice age?" Finn asked.

"Yes, son." Dr. Powers shook his head. "If this chart is correct, the rogue planet in our solar system is almost the size of Mars. Its gravity is pulling us away from the sun, into the cold of space. And it's not going to stop."

Did that mean what Eleanor feared it did? That the Freeze would never end? That the world would continue to grow colder until it became a lifeless ball of ice just floating through space?

"Look at the date, Simon," her mother said. "Skinner has had this star chart since the beginning of the Freeze. He *knows* about this. He knows why the earth has left its orbit, and he hasn't said anything about it!"

"How has he kept this a secret?" Julian asked.

"Maybe it's like the dark energy," Eleanor said. "Maybe it's like the Concentrator. Maybe it's meant for different eyes, and we can't really detect it. Just its gravity."

"But—" Julian sounded angry. "Everyone in the world has been asking why the Freeze is happening, and Skinner knew the entire time? That's just—"

"Skinner can't be the only one who knows," Eleanor's mother said.

"No," Dr. Powers said. "He can't. This *has* to go all the way to the top. Probably the UN. It's a cover-up on a massive scale."

"But why?" Julian asked.

"To preserve order, I would guess." Dr. Powers sighed. "To keep the peace. To preserve life. If Skinner knows about the rogue planet, then he must also know what that means for our world. It's no wonder he wants the energy here so badly."

"I almost can't blame him," her mother said, returning her attention to the Sync.

Rogue planets. Aliens on earth ten thousand years

ago. Dark energy. The end of the world. This was all too overwhelming. Eleanor had to stop and repeat to herself what had been said, to make sure she had understood everything.

"Sweetie," her mother said, "what's this?"

"What?" Eleanor asked.

"This message you sent. These are the coordinates I gave you. Who did you send them to?"

"You," Eleanor said.

Her mother frowned, appearing confused.

"Remember?" Eleanor said. "You contacted me when we were lost on the ice. I sent the coordinates back to you. It was the only way I could tell you where we were."

Her mother's sunburned cheeks paled. "Eleanor, I don't have my Sync."

"You don't? But I thought—"

"After I erased my data," her mother said, "I left my empty Sync in our camp."

In their camp? The abandoned camp Skinner had found? But that would mean—

"Oh no," Eleanor said.

"It was Skinner," her mother said.

Guilt tore through Eleanor's chest. Her mother had entrusted her with that information. Eleanor *had* protected it, until last night when she had sent the

251

coordinates to the very person her mother had tried to hide them from.

"I thought it was you," Eleanor whispered.

"Oh, honey . . . ," her mother began.

"That's exactly what Skinner wanted you to think," Dr. Powers said. "He played you like he's been playing the whole damn world."

"He may have the coordinates," Eleanor's mother said, "but he doesn't know about this place down here." She reached and touched Eleanor's cheek with the back of her hand. "It's not your fault," she whispered.

"Your mother is right," Dr. Powers said. "Skinner doesn't know about the fissure, and it's a good quarter mile from the coordinates, on the other side of the cavern. He'll be here soon. Any moment, perhaps, but he'll get to the site and think he has to drill through the ice. That'll buy us some time."

Time for what? Even without Skinner, the Concentrator was still gathering the earth's energy, while above them somewhere a rogue planet drew closer with its dark gravity, pulling the world into a frozen grave.

They had dinner with Amarok's village again that evening. Eleanor's mother and Dr. Powers tried to talk to Amarok about the Concentrator but arrived at the same conclusion that Eleanor had already come to—that the device was of very ancient origin. It seemed impossible to her that the Concentrator and the rogue planet weren't connected in some way. Eleanor could sense it just as clearly as she could sense that pervasive hum.

She wondered if Amarok's tribe could feel it. Or was it like those people who lived under power lines? Eventually, they just got used to the buzzing. Something about these Paleolithic people certainly felt different. It was like they crackled, especially gathered together as they were here. What had the energy of the Concentrator done to them? It had given them life, but at what price?

After they'd all finished eating, Amarok's village replayed the ritual of the previous night, but this time some of the villagers took turns telling stories. The tales pulled Eleanor's thoughts away from the Concentrator, and even in a different language, something about each of them felt familiar. She wasn't sure whether she just imagined it, but there always seemed to be a hero, and a struggle, as though all stories were the same in the end.

As the fire burned low, Amarok finally took the stage and told a tale of his own. Eleanor heard him say *"tawkeeshick"* and realized he was telling a story about the Concentrator. Did they know its inexplicable power had brought them back to life? Eleanor imagined a day, many generations from that night, when Amarok's people might have a new myth of their creation, the story of their birth from the black tree, and she wondered if the myth they told now was any less true than that.

Eleanor felt conflicted about the Concentrator. A part of her was terrified of it and wanted never to go near it. But another part of her wanted to understand it and was even drawn to it. No, pulled toward it, almost against her will. It was the key to everything. To the Freeze, the rogue planet, all of it. She had to see it again, as much as it frightened her.

Eleanor rose to her feet.

Sitting nearby, her mother asked, "Where are you going?"

"A walk," Eleanor said. "Just need to stretch my legs."

Her mom nodded. "Don't go far."

Eleanor ducked away, the glow of firelight at her back. It was night in the cavern now, just as it was on the surface. The sunlight that normally found its way down here through the glacier, following hidden facets of ice, had been replaced by starlight, turning the veins of gold to silver. The communal fire pit burned red behind her at the center of the village, the silhouetted villagers gathered around it.

Eleanor turned away from them toward the tundra and walked. It felt good to breathe the chilly air. It felt good to walk on the tundra's grass and moss.

"Hey, wait up!" Eleanor turned as Finn ran to join her. "Is it okay if I walk with you?" he asked.

She shrugged. "I guess."

"Where are we going?"

"If you want to walk with me, don't ask."

He held up his hands. "Okay, then."

The cavern sounds filled the following silence—the drip of water, the hollow breeze coming out of the canyon on the far side, and the voices from the village growing distant.

The hum was there, too. That same vibration, growing stronger as she crossed the tundra, tugging at her as though she had stepped into a river.

"You seriously don't feel that?" she said.

"Feel what?"

"That . . . hum."

He looked around. "Nope."

"I think it's the telluric current," she said. "I think I can feel it."

Before Finn could respond to that, a low, familiar

rumble shook the ground. The smell of musk. Then one of the boulders seemed to dislodge itself from the ground.

"Kixi," Eleanor whispered.

The woolly mammoth came toward them, a presence Eleanor sensed rather than saw, until she caught the glint in the animal's eyes and felt a blast of hot breath from her trunk.

Eleanor stopped and held still. "Hello, gorgeous."

The tip of Kixi's trunk found her again, her cheek this time, then moved down to her shoulder, then her arm, to her hand, which Eleanor cupped around the end of the dry, velvet nose.

"It's kind of crazy," Finn said. "She is literally the only one of her kind on the whole planet."

"She's all alone." Eleanor felt a sudden squeezing in her throat, which turned into a little sob before she could stop it. But she got it under control, sniffed, and wiped her nose, and then Kixi lifted her trunk to Eleanor's face again, touching a cheek now wet with tears. "I'm sorry," Eleanor whispered. "I'm sorry you're alone."

More than anyone or anything Eleanor had ever encountered, Kixi did not belong. She shouldn't be here. None of this should be here. And when Skinner and his scientists found what they were looking for down here, what then? She didn't know what the G.E.T. would do with the Concentrator once they found it, but felt she could safely assume it would mean the end of Kixi, and Amarok, and his whole tribe. Their home and way of life would be taken from them, and who knew what the loss of the energy from the Concentrator would mean for them?

"Good girl," Eleanor said. "You magnificent girl, Kixi. I won't let them do it. I promise." Then she turned away and resumed her trek across the tundra.

"Where are we going?" Finn asked.

"What did I say about asking that question?"

"Sorry. It just . . . seems like we're heading to the Concentrator."

"We are," Eleanor said.

"Why?"

"Because that's where this all started."

They reached that same hill, climbed it, and looked down at the crater. The humming in Eleanor's mind had become deafening again, the black structure almost quivering with its energy.

She sat down on the turf and stared at the Concentrator, trying to fix it in place in her mind and truly see it. She stopped fighting the humming and just let it pass through her, imagining it reaching down to her marrow. She closed her eyes, slowed her breathing, and relaxed. As she did, the humming acquired a definite direction, a movement. She felt it sweeping through her, around her, from all directions.

She let her mind get swept up by it, and it carried her down the hill, into the crater, to the structure at its heart. The Concentrator's branches gathered her up, rolling her like a spider wrapping its prey, folding her tighter and tighter around herself until she broke apart, dissolving into something gossamer and insubstantial, then shuttled her up, up, up to its peak.

From there, the Concentrator launched her skyward at blinding speed. She shot up through the cavern, toward its ceiling, but instead of crashing into it, she passed through, tunneling to the surface of the ice sheet, and blasted into the sky. The earth's horizon gained curvature as she left it behind, flying a prescribed path into the vacuum of space.

That was when she saw her destination.

A black planet, pulling her in.

Immense. Dark. Impossible for Eleanor to fully take in or comprehend. If the Concentrator in the cavern had been built for eyes adapted to a different world, then *this* was a world that would make such sight necessary. Its twisted surface, encrusted with baffling and hideous towers and monuments, repelled Eleanor, and when she attempted to contemplate what kind of life might exist on this rogue world, a suffocating horror seized her, digging its dirty fingers into her mind, reaching inward for the deepest part of her.

She screamed.

"Eleanor, wake up!"

She opened her eyes, back on the tundra, sitting above the Concentrator. Finn knelt in front of her, holding her by the shoulders.

"Finn?" she said.

"What *was* that?" He looked down with a forceful sigh. "The Concentrator was making all kinds of sounds, and you were . . . just gone."

For a moment, she thought the humming had stopped, but then she realized she could still feel it, if she tuned in. It was just that now she found she could filter it out when she wanted. "Yes, I was gone," she said.

"Gone where?"

She looked up at the cavern's ceiling high above. "I know how the Concentrator and the rogue planet are connected."

WHEN SHE TOLD HER MOM AND DR. POWERS WHAT SHE had seen, they listened with concern but didn't seem ready to accept it. Visions, it seemed, fell fairly low in reliability on the scale of empirical evidence.

"It was real, Mom," Eleanor said. "I know it."

"Dreams can be that way," her mother said. "I have no doubt it felt real to you. But—"

"It didn't *feel* real, it *was* real. I can't explain it."

"Try," Finn said. He had been there with her and seemed the most ready to believe.

Eleanor thought about it a moment. "It's like the rogue planet is harvesting telluric currents through the

Concentrator, which is converting it to dark energy. Almost like it's a vampire or something. I think that's why they're both here." And if the Concentrator had really been there for as long as Amarok said it had, that meant the alien beings who had created it had planned this a very, very long time ago. Tens of thousands of years.

Something boomed above them, a distant thunder that reverberated through the cavern walls. Eleanor looked up, as did everyone else in the hut.

Eleanor's mother covered her mouth. "It's Skinner," she said. "He's here."

When the second peal sounded, voices cried out elsewhere in the village. This was something Amarok's people had not yet adapted to, the sounds of modern machinery tearing into the ice sheet overhead.

Eleanor's mother and Dr. Powers left the hut, and Eleanor followed after them with Julian and Finn. They found Amarok at the center of the village, next to the communal fire still burning low. In the next few moments, his people gathered to him, and he lifted his hands high.

His voice rumbled over his villagers, quieting them. Then he began smoothly pointing his fingers, calling out certain men and women. It looked like he was assigning tasks, a force for calm and order.

Dr. Powers spoke in a murmur. "We need to see what's up there."

"Are you sure we should risk it?" her mother asked. "If we're spotted, if we reveal the crevasse . . ."

"The cover of night should keep us hidden. We have to know what to expect, Sam."

"You're right. The kids can stay—"

"No way," Eleanor said.

"Honey, it could be dangerous," her mom said. "We don't know what Skinner is planning."

"I traveled all the way to the Arctic, and I am *not* letting you out of my sight. No. Way."

Her mom opened her mouth as if to protest again, but closed it and nodded. They returned to their hut as the rest of the villagers dispersed. The periodic booming continued to penetrate the cavern, still somewhat dull and remote. They gathered their polar masks from among the mammoth bones, listening to it. Eleanor tried counting the seconds between blasts, which seemed to occur every three to five minutes.

After they had all suited up, they left the hut and headed through the village, in the opposite direction from the Concentrator. On the way, Amarok found them. He had dressed in additional layers of fur and once again carried his spear.

262

"We go up," he said, and fell in with them.

They left the village behind and crossed another stretch of rolling ground, heading toward the cavern wall. As they drew near it, Eleanor noticed a narrow slot of a canyon and, next to its entrance, a couple of sleds. Amarok let out a shrill whistle, and from across the tundra, his wolves came streaking toward them, blurs of gray, brown, and black.

Their speed took Eleanor's breath, as did their size when they got closer. Their broad heads reached as high as her chest, and she didn't think she could even wrap her arms around their thick necks. Not that she was in a hurry to try. They circled Amarok, tongues out, ears partly back, each waiting for him to acknowledge them, which he did with a pat on the head or a rub behind the ear. There were ten of them.

"You are looking at some of the first domesticated dogs in the world," her mother said.

"Dogs?" Finn said.

"The difference between a dog and a wolf is more behavioral than genetic," Dr. Powers said. "These animals are still a long way from Lassie, but they're tame."

Amarok called each of the wolves by name and harnessed them to one of the sleds. They pawed the ground, panting, bristling with energy. When they were all in place, Amarok mounted the back of the sled and motioned for Eleanor and the others to climb on.

"They can pull all of us?" she asked.

"And more," her mother said.

They settled down on the flatbed of the sled, which was made from wood and bone, bound together by leather cords, and covered in furs. Amarok shouted a command to the wolves, and they surged as a single, sudden wave. The sled leaped forward.

Amarok took them into the canyon, its sheer ice walls rising up, layer upon layer, striations of impenetrable depth in shades of blue and white. The changing angles of the walls blocked any view of the canyon's upper limits. Eleanor could barely see more than a few turns ahead as Amarok guided them inward.

The panting of the wolves and the hiss of the sled's passage echoed back to them. The animals' shoulders and haunches undulated in a wave of frosty fur as the floor of the canyon inclined upward, and the sled climbed.

Up they rose, from the glacier's deepest bones and ligaments, through its muscles, toward its skin. Eleanor's eyes teared up in the icy rush of air, and the higher the sled reached, the colder it became.

The canyon turned and bent back on itself, cutting a jagged path, but Amarok took the sled along its course with ease, the communication between him and his wolves natural and subtle, a language of primal utterances that sounded as if it emerged from a shared consciousness.

"You'll need to put your masks on soon," Dr. Powers said. "We're nearing the surface."

"The power is out in our suits," Finn said.

"Ours, too," his father said. "But they'll still offer you some protection for the brief exposure."

Eleanor put her mask on, and so did the others. A few minutes later, Amarok brought the sled to a graceful stop. A sharp wedge of night sky sliced the canyon open above them, filled with stars. Eleanor felt the cold like a waterfall pouring over the lip of the canyon, crashing down on her, and a wind howled in like air blown over a bottle.

The wolves huffed, and a few of them yawned with high-pitched whines. Eleanor wondered how they could survive up here. Or Amarok, for that matter. She decided it must be another effect of the Concentrator's energy. In addition to reviving people and animals, it made them more robust, somehow.

"We'll leave the dogs here," Dr. Powers said. "Let's stay quiet."

Amarok nodded and gave an order to his wolves, and they lay down as one. Dr. Powers then led their party in the final ascent of the crevasse, slowing to a crawl as they reached the surface.

Dr. Powers and Amarok stuck their heads up first, an inch at a time. "My God," Dr. Powers whispered.

"What is it?" Eleanor's mother asked.

He motioned them up.

Eleanor climbed until she, too, could see over the edge, across the surface. The storm had departed from the ice sheet, as predicted, and curtains of aurora waved across the sky. The glacier's expanse spread even farther to the horizon than before. Flat, desolate, pale in the moonlight, and unbroken.

Except for the spheres.

Polaris Station marched toward them out of the night. The towering pods thundered across the ice sheet on their hydraulic legs, seeming unstoppable, one slow and heavy footfall at a time, spotlights flooding their path, their many windows like the glowing eyes of a monolithic insect. Eleanor fought the urge to duck from their sight.

"I've never seen them mobile," Eleanor's mother whispered.

"The G.E.T. doesn't mess around," Dr. Powers said. "It looks like they're almost in position over the Concentrator."

"How long after they start drilling until they breach

the cavern?" her mother asked.

"Depends on the equipment they've got—I've never seen the station's drills operational. They won't start until morning, at any rate."

Eleanor noticed Amarok, the expression on his face one of awe and horror. What could he be thinking? Were the spheres like magic to him? Demons? She thought about his village below, their world about to end for the second time, destroyed by something perhaps more inexplicable to them than the ice age had been.

They couldn't let that happen. "We have to stop them," Eleanor said.

"How're we going to do that?" Julian asked.

"I don't know. There's got to be someone we can contact. Someone—"

"There isn't," Dr. Powers said. "The G.E.T. and Skinner are too powerful. They've got the UN behind them."

"Then we evacuate the village," her mother asked. "Like we talked about."

"No," Amarok said.

Everyone turned to look at him. The earlier fear on his face had been replaced by a ferocious resolve, and Eleanor glimpsed the Stone Age warrior he had once been and still was. The way he gripped his spear, she could imagine him facing down a polar bear.

"No?" Eleanor's mother said. "Amarok, these—"

"No," Amarok said again, baring his teeth like one of his wolves. "Our home. We *fight*."

Her mother paced around the mammoth-bone hut. "This is suicide! When Amarok and his warriors attack Polaris Station, they will do so with arrows. *Sticks and stones*. Skinner and his hired security will have guns."

She was right. Amarok had no hope. This was the Stone Age versus the twenty-first century, and history had already decided the victor. Amarok just didn't know it yet.

"We should just evacuate the cavern," her mother said.

"You're asking them to abandon their home," Dr. Powers said. "Their *world*. Where would they go?"

"I don't know! But a slim chance is better than no chance."

Amarok and his warriors were somewhere in the village, preparing for their assault. Since he had first announced his intentions up at the surface, a cold dread had been growing in Eleanor's chest. The futility of the attack wasn't even a question, and the nobility or poetry or whatever did nothing to assuage the tragedy of it.

Dr. Powers shook his head. "This isn't your choice, Sam. You aren't in charge of these people. They have the right to decide for themselves how they want to face this."

"They are cavemen, Simon! They haven't adapted to the modern world. They aren't ready to decide something like this. You may think it arrogant, but I know better than they do."

"Can you hear yourself?" Dr. Powers asked. "Let Amarok worry about his people, Sam. The only thing *we* need to worry about is what Skinner will do with the Concentrator."

"Maybe we can reason with him," her mother said. "Now that we know more about it, maybe he'll finally listen."

Eleanor had met Skinner, and even she knew that didn't seem likely. "What are you going to say, Mom? 'Hey, Skinner, this Concentrator thing is, like, ten thousand years old, and it's turning the earth's energy into dark energy, and oh, by the way, it was made by aliens, so leave it alone.' Because I think I can tell you what he'll say to that."

Her mother gave her a don't-be-ridiculous look. "I still don't know if *I* believe half of what you just said."

"But she has a point," Dr. Powers said. "You and I both know Skinner. How he is once he's made up his mind. And remember, now we know this is a man who has apparently participated in a lie to the entire world. He may even be the architect of it."

Eleanor's mother shook her head but spoke no word against that.

"But for the sake of argument," Dr. Powers said, "what *would* you say to him?"

"I . . ." Her mother spread her hands for a moment, as if waiting for the words to flock to her, but a few moments later, she let them drop with a sigh. "I guess I'd say what I said before. We don't understand the energy here nearly well enough to use it. It's too dangerous."

"And why would he listen this time?" Dr. Powers asked.

Her mother clenched her jaw.

"Sam?" Dr. Powers said.

"I don't know, Simon!" She was almost shaking. "I can barely accept what I've seen with my own eyes! I don't know if that . . . thing is our salvation or our destruction or what! All I do know is we have to do something to stop Skinner from getting his hands on it!"

Eleanor sidled closer to her mom and put an arm around her. "Mom, it's okay. We'll figure something out."

Dr. Powers softened. "I agree with you, Sam. We have to keep Skinner from getting into this cavern. He's facing the end of the world, and I think he's trying to hoard all the energy he can. From any source. I think he's desperate, and that makes him dangerous. Maybe as dangerous as the Concentrator."

── CHAPTER ──
21

A FEW HOURS LATER, THE VILLAGE HAD FINISHED ITS PREP-
arations for battle. Eleanor had stayed with her
mom, who was still pretty upset, while Dr. Powers had
gone out to help Amarok. When he returned, he stood
in the doorway of the hut, encircled by mammoth
bones. Eleanor couldn't read his expression. Regret?
Frustration? Determination? Perhaps all of that.

"The warriors are ready to move out," he finally
said. "Julian and Finn are with them. The Paleos have
a solid strategy. They just might pull this off."

Eleanor's mother nodded.

"Sam, are you really going to sit this out?" he asked.

Her mother nodded again.

"Well, I won't," he said. "I can't."

"That's fine for you. But what about your boys, Simon?"

"I gave them the choice," he said. "The same respect we owe to Amarok."

"What would their mother think, I wonder?"

"What's the alternative here?" Dr. Powers said. "Skinner will silence us one way or another for the secret we've uncovered, of that I have no doubt. He's got bounty hunters and thugs working for him, and we really don't know what he's capable of."

"He's nothing but a scientist turned bureaucrat," her mother said. "Stop exaggerating."

"What about Amarok?" Dr. Powers said. "Don't these people have the right to defend their home?"

"The men and women in that station are innocent," her mother said. "They're just following Skinner's orders, but Amarok and his people are about to kill them, or die trying."

That was a point Eleanor hadn't considered. She had met some of those people, like Dr. Grant.

"Will you still think they're innocent when they follow Skinner's orders to drive out Amarok's village?" Dr. Powers asked.

"You don't know that will happen."

"Oh yes, I do. And so do you. Skinner won't let the

fact that indigenous people live here stop him. He'll tear this cavern apart and claim the Concentrator, and that'll be it for them. But I'm not going to take it lying down, and I sure as hell won't tell Amarok to. So long, Sam." Dr. Powers marched from the hut.

Eleanor waited a few moments before speaking. She thought about everything that had been said on both sides of the argument. She thought about everything Skinner had done and would likely do. And she made up her mind. "I'm going with them," she said.

Her mother gasped. "What?"

"Mom, whatever that Concentrator is"—Eleanor pointed toward it with the accuracy of a compass, feeling the energy lines—"Skinner *cannot* get his hands on it. Ever."

Her mother stood. "Well, I *cannot* allow you to place yourself in harm's way!"

"Allow?" Eleanor rose to her feet. "Who're you kidding, Mom? I've been putting myself in harm's way for years. You can't stop me. Uncle Jack figured that out a long time ago. Where've you been?"

The question hung in the air like the echo of a slap to the face.

Her mother's gaze fell just a bit. "It's true I may not have always been there for you. But that's because I've been up here trying to save the human race, Eleanor.

Please stop acting like such a child for once."

Eleanor didn't have the time or patience to evaluate her mother's motives in that moment. The others were getting ready to march up the crevasse. "Just blame it on the Donor so I can get out of here."

Her mother's mouth snapped shut. She held her lips tight, and then she said, "I am your mother, and you belong here with me."

"You know what, Mom?" Eleanor said. "Did you ever stop to think that maybe you belong with *me*?" Then she stormed from the hut.

Outside, a column of Stone Age warriors, men and women alike, had begun its march toward the canyon. Amarok led them, while Dr. Powers brought up the rear with Finn and Julian. Eleanor trotted after them until she'd caught up, expecting, and maybe even hoping, to hear her mother calling after her.

But she didn't.

When she fell in with Dr. Powers, Finn, and Julian, they said nothing but simply gave her a grim nod, which she returned. When the column reached the entrance to the canyon, Amarok mounted his sled, which had been loaded up with cargo, some kind of lattice of wood and bone, and ordered his wolves forward. They flew into the canyon, and the column followed on foot.

Several hundred yards in, Eleanor wished she were

riding on that sled. The climb was arduous, though it seemed to barely faze the villagers. It took some time to reach the surface, and when they did, they found the ice sheet ablush with the coming dawn.

Eleanor put on her mask against the cold, while the villagers set to work with the lattices, stretching them out inside the crevasse. They were frameworks for animal skins and fur, specifically *white* skins and fur—seals, polar bears, and rabbits. These were hunting blinds, a camouflage, the same strategy the villagers had likely once used to take down game on the ice.

After Amarok's people had stretched the skins over the first blind, they slowly raised it out of the crevasse, up onto the glacier. Once it was in position, several men and women climbed up behind it, safely hidden, and began to push it forward a few inches at a time.

Those in the crevasse prepared another blind and sent it up, then another, and another, until they came to the last. Amarok had unharnessed his wolves from the sled. He gave them one last command to stay, then motioned for Dr. Powers, along with Eleanor, Finn, and Julian, to join him and the few remaining warriors behind the blind.

Up on the ice sheet, the brutal cold reminded Eleanor that her suit still had no power. But she warmed herself a bit pushing the heavy blind forward by increments with each silent order from Amarok.

At that careful pace, it took them another hour to cover the distance between the crevasse and the station, but before the sun broke over the horizon, all the warriors had reached their positions surrounding the station, hidden behind their blinds, armed with spears, bows, and clubs.

After that, they waited, and that was when Eleanor really began to feel the cold. It wasn't aggressive, like it had been during the storm; this felt more insidious, creeping up from below, like an invasive parasite waiting to take root in her if she stayed in one place for too long. Her teeth chattered. She shivered. So did Finn, Julian, and even Dr. Powers, but Amarok and his people appeared unaffected.

After the sun had risen, the hatch on the central sphere finally opened, and several crew members lowered a ladder and climbed down to the ice. They wore full polar gear, and Eleanor watched through cracks in the blind, wondering if one of them was Skinner. If so, all they'd need would be a single, well-placed arrow. But there wasn't any way to be sure, and they couldn't risk a premature attack. If they did, Skinner would just hole up in the sphere and call in reinforcements, and that would be the end of Amarok's people.

The crew members walked around the site with

various sensors and other equipment, taking measurements and collecting data. Eleanor could sense the Concentrator directly below them, emitting its stolen energy, and felt the weight of the rogue world pressing down from the sky above.

The crew members conferred for some time, seemed to come to some kind of decision, and then hammered a series of poles and stakes into the ice. Shortly after that, the spheres disgorged the rest of their occupants. Dozens of additional men and women moved about beneath the station, opening compartments around the bases of the spheres, and an inner machinery awoke. The spheres ejected huge pieces of themselves, which Eleanor assumed would be assembled into a drill.

Then she saw Boar. He walked among the crew without assisting, simply observing, like some kind of terrifying overseer.

In terms of numbers, Amarok's people were evenly matched with the G.E.T. But Eleanor noticed that the crew had a few security guards placed among them, and they had pistols holstered at their hips or strapped to their thighs, while others carried rifles.

Amarok adjusted his stance, about to give the order to attack, and Eleanor felt the cool rush of adrenaline shoot through her veins. She tried to calm herself, but her breathing deepened and her pulse quickened. The battle was about to begin.

Amarok gave those behind his blind a lip-curled smile, and then bellowed a single word.

His people responded with instant, deafening shouts and shrieks, simultaneously launching a barrage from their projectile weapons.

The station crew panicked, ducking and scattering as the sound and the missiles fell upon them. A few of them went down, pierced by arrows or spears, but a moment later, the crew seemed to collectively recover and regroup from the surprise of the attack.

"Get down," Dr. Powers said.

Eleanor went flat against the ice, and a second later, bullets ripped through the blind, the loud crack of gunfire ringing in her ears. Amarok turned back toward the fissure, gave a shrill whistle, then jumped up and charged. All his people followed his lead in a great rush, closing the distance between them and the crew.

The gunfire escalated, and Eleanor watched in horror for the next few moments as many of the villagers jerked and fell in splashes of blood. But those who made it in took the fighting hand-to-hand, and here, Amarok's people proved to be superior. They grappled the crew to the ground, breaking bones, choking, slicing. It was savage, and Eleanor wanted to look away.

Then something gray streaked past the blind from behind her. Then another, and another. Amarok's wolves. They'd been summoned to battle, and they flew snarling into the fight, lithe and lethal, taking G.E.T. crew down by their arms and throats.

But the guns continued to fire, and men, women, and wolves screamed. Dr. Powers twisted his grip on a club Amarok had given him. "I'm going in," he said. "I'll try to get a pistol."

Then he scrambled up and rushed forward with the same ferocity as the villagers. Eleanor watched him dive and weave, swinging his weapon like a bat. He caught a couple of the crew with solid blows, but before he could get his hands on a firearm, Boar crashed into him and he went down hard. Then the giant grabbed him by the throat.

"NO!" Julian howled, and a second later, he and Finn were racing in.

Eleanor followed them, almost without thinking, and found herself suddenly in the midst of the battle.

Dr. Powers thrashed and pummeled Boar, who still had him pinned to the ground by the throat, but his blows had no effect, and he was clearly weakening.

Julian flew at the giant with his own club, bashing his head and shoulders, forcing Boar to let go of Dr. Powers to shield himself. Dr. Powers scrambled away just as the giant grabbed Julian's club midblow and threw it back at him, knocking him to the ground.

Dr. Powers had regained his club and went in for a swing, but Boar swung his fist first, cracking the side of Dr. Powers's head. Eleanor heard the impact, and Dr. Powers wobbled down to his knees.

Finn screamed, "DAD!" and raised his own weapon, but before he could charge, Amarok leaped between him and Boar.

The giant looked down as Amarok adjusted his spear. The fighting around the two came to a halt as both sides paused to watch what would happen. Boar scooped up a club, swung it a few times as if testing its weight, and then assumed a wide stance.

Three of Amarok's wolves appeared at his side, but he ordered them back. He and Boar then circled each other for a few moments. When Boar launched his attack, Amarok ducked and dodged the giant's blows, each time barely avoiding them. Amarok then went in for a strike, and Boar deflected the spear thrust with the club.

For several minutes, the two of them fought as equals, swinging, dodging, thrusting, blocking. Both were breathing hard, Boar through his mask, Amarok in the open air.

But then one of the giant's blows glanced off

Amarok's side. The warrior cried out and stumbled, dropping his spear. Boar seized the opportunity and pounced, but Amarok ducked out of the way into a roll, snatched up his spear, and hurled it.

The razor spearhead caught Boar square in the chest and buried itself to the shaft. The giant looked down at the red stain spreading through the white of his polar-bear fur. Then he dropped to his knees with a moan and fell on his back.

Those who had watched the fight remained motionless in the aftermath. Eleanor wondered if that had ended the battle, these two champions dueling for the fate of them all. Amarok looked as though he was about to say something, but before he could, a single gunshot exploded, knocking him to the ground.

Eleanor cried out. The bullet had hit him in the shoulder, and he lay on the ice, growling and grunting in pain.

The man who had fired the shot spoke. "I see Dr. Powers and his sons. I see Miss Perry. But I do not see Dr. Perry."

It was Skinner. Eleanor recognized his voice through his mask, and as he spoke, his crew seemed to regain themselves, while Amarok's fall seemed to have shocked and weakened the resolve of his people. Even Amarok's wolves appeared submissive and unsure, ears back, whining and licking their master's face and wound. In the next few moments, those security forces still standing lifted their guns and aimed them at the stunned warriors.

"You have attacked a legally sanctioned installation operating under the authority of the Global Energy Trust and the United Nations," Skinner said. "I suggest an orderly surrender, unless more of you want to die."

The Paleos probably hadn't understood any of that, but when Skinner fired a warning shot into the air, they dropped their spears and clubs.

Skinner nodded and then walked toward Eleanor. "Miss Perry, where is your mother?"

"She's dead," Eleanor said, without hesitation.

"Your demeanor suggests otherwise. You and this army of yours did not simply materialize on the ice. You came from somewhere." Skinner swiveled his masked face from side to side, appearing to scrutinize the Stone Age warriors. "Upper Paleolithic, if I am not mistaken. Fascinating. And impossible."

"Guess you don't know everything," Eleanor said.

"You are right about that." Skinner pointed his gun at Finn's head. "Miss Perry, where is your mother? And do not even consider lying to me again, or Mr. Powers here will pay."

CHAPTER
22

"NO!" Dr. Powers cried. "Skinner, he's a child!" Eleanor panicked. "She's in the village! Please! Just— just don't shoot!"

Finn was shaking so hard, Eleanor could see it through all his layers of gear.

"Village?" Skinner said. "What village?"

"PLEASE!" Eleanor shouted. "Take the gun away!"

"Answer my question, Miss Perry." Skinner extended the barrel even closer to Finn. "What village?"

"*Their* village!" Eleanor's voice deteriorated. "Under the ice sheet."

Skinner held still for several moments without

speaking, the gun unwavering. "Show me," he finally said, turning the gun on her.

Eleanor nodded her acquiescence, glad Finn was no longer in danger, then bowed her head as she led the way toward the fissure. She felt Amarok's people watching her, and she betrayed them with every step, passed the wounded and the dead, men, women, and wolves. But what else could she do? The battle was lost.

Skinner gave an order to one of his men. "Keep them here until I return. Take no chances. If they give you trouble, shoot them."

"Yes, sir."

Skinner pressed the gun to Eleanor's back. "Let's go, Miss Perry. Just you and me."

They left Polaris Station behind and crossed the quarter mile of ice. As they approached the fissure, Dr. Skinner shook his head. "I should have noticed this before. Where does it lead?"

"All the way down," Eleanor said.

They climbed down in silence, passing Amarok's empty sled. At the sight of it, all Eleanor could think was that her mother had been right. It had been suicide to think the villagers could make a stand against the modern world and prevail.

After they had descended some distance, Skinner spoke up. "I must say, I'm surprised to see you alive, Miss Perry. After our last communication, I'd been expecting to find a corpse waiting at those coordinates. You seemed to be in bad shape."

At the reminder of his deception, a spark of anger ignited in Eleanor, lighting a path through her despair and defeat. She followed its heat, coaxing it to life. "What did you do to Luke?" she asked.

"Mr. Fournier? He escaped right after you did. Fled to Barrow, I believe."

At least he was alive and unharmed.

"I know about the rogue planet," Eleanor said.

Skinner sighed. "That is unfortunate. Your silence is critical, Miss Perry."

"So you're going to kill me? Kill my mom? Kill everyone who finds out about it?"

"Don't be absurd," he said. "You will all be given the opportunity to adopt the Preservation Protocol."

"Preservation Protocol?" Eleanor remembered that name from her science class, the conspiracy theory Mr. Fiske had dismissed. So it was real. "Is this what you call *preservation*?"

"You waste my time, Miss Perry."

"How?"

"You lack the maturity to understand."

"I understand perfectly well that you have a gun to my back."

"You think I am evil," Skinner said. "But I am safe-guarding human life on this planet in a systematic way that maximizes its chances at a meaningful survival. Millions have died as a result of this ice age. Billions will follow. What does your life amount to among them? The relative value of a single life is insignificant when compared—"

"My life is NOT insignificant!" Eleanor stopped and spun around to face him. He still held the gun, but she didn't care. "My mom's life is not insignificant! Neither is Uncle Jack's! Or Finn's! They all deserve to know! They deserve the chance to fight—"

"NO!" Skinner bellowed. "Human beings are not equipped to handle this threat! If it had been left to the population at large, our world would already be in a state of chaos with ZERO chance of survival!"

His argument sounded familiar. It echoed the discussion between Eleanor's mother and Dr. Powers over Amarok's decision to fight for his home against the spheres of Polaris Station. Skinner almost sounded like her mom.

"Has anyone gone up there?" Eleanor asked.

"Where?" Skinner asked.

"To the rogue world."

He sighed. "You make my point for me, Miss Perry. Why would we waste our diminishing energy resources on a pointless mission to a lifeless, uninhabitable world? If you were in charge, we'd—"

"It isn't uninhabited," Eleanor said.

"Pardon me?"

"I won't, but what I said is that the rogue world isn't uninhabited."

He snorted. "Don't be ridiculous."

Eleanor wished she could see his face to know if he was being sincere. Could it be that he didn't know? Perhaps he didn't. Perhaps no one did.

"Miss Perry," he said, adopting a condescending tone, "rogue worlds travel the harsh vacuum of space. They are orphans, without a parent star to give them energy and create the conditions to sustain life. They are *dead* by definition."

Eleanor turned away from him and resumed her descent. Perhaps if he saw the Concentrator, he would understand. Perhaps if he realized what the earth faced, he would stop what he was doing. Amarok and his people couldn't fight the G.E.T., but perhaps Eleanor could change their course.

"You need to see something," she said.

When they reached the end of the canyon, and the cavern opened wide, Skinner's even, calculated demeanor finally slipped, if only for a moment. "My God," he whispered. "I've never seen anything like this."

Eleanor pulled off her mask. "It's warm down here," she said. "You won't need your gear."

Skinner removed his mask too. "Those huts up ahead," he said. "They appear to be constructed of mammoth bones."

"They are," Eleanor said. "That's Amarok's village."

"Who is this Amarok you keep mentioning?"

"He's the man you shot," Eleanor said, filling each word with venom.

"Where is your mother?"

"I told you, in the village."

"Do you know the location of the energy signature?"

"On the other side of the cavern."

"Take me there."

Eleanor led him past Amarok's other sled, between the mammoth-bone huts, to the center of the village, where Skinner stopped and called, "Dr. Perry? Come out, please! I have your daughter!"

Eleanor watched the flap of their hut from the corner of her eye, waiting for her mother to emerge. She didn't.

"Dr. Perry!" Skinner shouted.

Silence. Still no sign of her mom. Eleanor wondered where she could have gone. They would have passed

289

her if she'd come up the crevasse.

Skinner jabbed Eleanor in the ribs with his gun. "I believe you have lied to me, Miss Perry."

"This is where she was when I left," Eleanor said. "I swear."

"Hmm." He narrowed his eyes. "Then take me to the energy source. If you have lied to me, your liability will have exceeded your usefulness."

Eleanor felt a fresh surge of fear. Without her mom, she was alone down here with this man. He could shoot her, at any moment, in the name of preservation.

"It's this way," she said, and led him onto the tundra.

As they walked, he remarked on the vegetation, the geological features, the smell of the air. "This entire cavern is an ice age time capsule," he said. "How is this possible?"

Eleanor wondered where Kixi was but willed silently for her to stay there, out of Skinner's sight. "It's an effect of the Concentrator," she said.

"Is that what Dr. Perry named the energy source?"

"Yes," Eleanor said.

Before long, they arrived at the final hill. As they reached its crest and looked down into the crater, Eleanor saw her mother standing at the base of the Concentrator.

"Mom!" she shouted. "Run!"

"Eleanor?" her mother called "What—?" But then she saw Skinner, and the gun, and she paled.

"Stay where you are, Dr. Perry," Skinner said.

Eleanor's mother nodded. "Aaron, what are you doing? That's my daughter."

"Everyone has daughters," Skinner said, walking Eleanor down the slope. "Everyone has sons. Or a mother, or cousins, or a husband, or a best friend. Your relationship warrants no special status."

When they reached the base of the crater, Skinner shoved Eleanor toward her mother, who caught her in her arms. They hugged for a moment.

"I'm sorry," Eleanor whispered.

"No, sweetie," her mother said. "I—"

"A Concentrator, you called this?" Skinner still had the gun pointed at them, but he was looking upward into the shifting, impenetrable branches.

"Yes," her mother said. "This is what has been concentrating the telluric currents."

"Ley lines." Skinner shook his head with a huff. "Who would've thought?"

"Aaron, please listen to me." Eleanor's mother let go of her and took a hesitant step toward Skinner, hands up in front of her. She was about to try reasoning with him after all. "This is not a source of energy."

"Really?" he said. "Because I just measured it from the surface, and I can assure you this is most definitely a source of energy."

"No," her mother said. "You don't understand. This is *the* energy. The earth's. Calling it a resource would be like calling your blood or your DNA a resource. Remove it, and you die."

"The earth is already dying," Skinner said, gaze roaming back up the trunk of the Concentrator, voice becoming absent. "But if we are clever, some may survive."

"The earth isn't dying," her mother said. "It's hemorrhaging. Right here, where this object is embedded. But we can stop it—"

"Stop it?" Skinner said. "Quite the opposite, Dr. Perry; we need to exploit it while we can. Where is the wasted energy going now?"

"To the rogue planet," Eleanor said. "That's what I tried telling you before. That planet up there isn't just pulling the earth out of orbit. It's stealing the earth's energy."

"How do you know this?" Skinner asked.

Eleanor lifted her chin. "I've . . . seen it. In my mind."

Skinner smirked at Eleanor. "Is that so?" Then he turned to Eleanor's mom. "Do you concur with your esteemed colleague's psychic assessment, Dr. Skinner?"

Her mom's back stiffened. "Don't you *dare* mock my daughter."

"Look at that thing!" Eleanor pointed at the Concentrator. "Does that look natural to you? It's been here for thousands of years! And someone—something—put it here!"

Skinner paused. He appeared to be thinking about Eleanor's statement. "I grant there are unanswered questions, Miss Perry. But nothing that you have said changes the fundamentals of our situation."

"What fundamentals?" Eleanor asked.

"The invading world will continue to pull the earth out of orbit," Skinner said. "The earth will continue to freeze. Our *only* hope is the plan I conceived when I first discovered the rogue planet: to stockpile enough energy for a handful of humans to survive until the rogue planet has moved out of our solar system and our orbit has corrected itself. You see, Miss Perry, that is what rogue planets do. They roam. They move on."

"Not *this* rogue planet," Eleanor said.

"That is an absurd proposition, Miss Perry. Are you really suggesting that someone is up there steering an entire planet as though it were a car, stopping to fill up at our pump?"

When he said it that way, Eleanor heard the

absurdity in it and had no reply.

"This site presents an unparalleled opportunity," Dr. Skinner said. "To stop it, as your mother suggests—" He paused. Then he looked hard at Eleanor's mom. "What did you mean by that, Dr. Perry? What exactly were you doing here when we arrived?"

Eleanor's mother took a step back. "I was trying to shut it down."

"To what end?"

"If we can somehow disable it, we can stop the hemorrhaging. We can save the earth's energy."

"But I *will* save the earth's energy—"

"No, Aaron, not your way," her mother said. "And I'm not giving up. I'll go to the press. I have evidence. You won't get away with this lie anymore."

"I see." Skinner looked up at the cavern's ceiling for several moments and then nodded once to himself, firmly. "Dr. Perry, you and your daughter have been deemed imminent threats to the Global Energy Trust and the success of the UN's Preservation Protocol. Please move back up the hill."

The way he said it made it sound like some kind of official pronouncement.

"Imminent threats?" Eleanor's mother said. "What does *that* mean? You—"

"Dr. Perry, please move up the hill," Skinner said.

"Aaron, you—"

"Now!"

Eleanor flinched. So did her mother. They stepped away from the Concentrator and walked out of the crater. Skinner followed behind them.

When they reached the top of the hill, Skinner said, "Keep walking."

"Why?" her mother said, turning around. "Where are we going?"

"I am putting some distance between you and the Concentrator," he said, his pistol unwavering.

Dr. Powers had said they didn't know what Skinner was capable of. He had already shot Amarok. Was he going to shoot them? At that thought, Eleanor's legs weakened, and she almost lost her footing.

Her mother folded her arms and widened her stance. "I'm not going anywhere. This is ridiculous. What happened to you, Aaron? You used to be a scientist. What are you doing with a gun?"

"You are a talented scientist yourself, Dr. Perry," Skinner said. "I'd much rather you joined me. But since you've made it perfectly clear that won't be possible, I need you to turn around now."

Panic leaped through Eleanor.

Her mother swallowed.

"Do as I say, Dr. Perry."

"Why?" Her mother's voice quavered.

"Please," Skinner said. "Do as I—"

"Why?" Her mother's voice pitched higher. "You can't—"

"TURN AROUND!" Skinner shouted.

Her mother did what he asked, her eyes filled with fear as they made contact with Eleanor's.

"Mom?" Eleanor couldn't think of anything she could do to stop this. Was he about to—

"Please, Aaron," her mother said. "Whatever you do to me, don't hurt my daughter, she's innocent—"

"Silence." Skinner reached into one of his pockets and pulled out a plastic zip tie. "I won't hurt anyone unless I have to. Hands behind your back, please."

Her mother closed her eyes and reached her hands backward. Skinner cinched them together at the wrists with the zip tie. Then he turned to Eleanor.

"Now you, Miss Perry."

Eleanor did as her mother had done.

"Sit down," Skinner said. "Both of you."

Eleanor and her mother lowered themselves to the ground, backs to each other, sitting cross-legged. Skinner pulled a handheld radio out from another pocket in his suit.

The device chirped. "This is Skinner. Status update? Over."

A staticky voice came through the radio. "The hostiles are secure. Medical attention underway."

"Casualties?" Skinner asked.

"Four dead. Fifteen wounded."

"Medical status of the hostiles?"

"Comparable casualties."

"See to their medical needs as well," Skinner said. "After that, resume preparation for drilling. There is a crevasse a quarter mile away, but I don't think it will provide efficient access."

"Yes, sir."

"There is a cavern directly below the station. I estimate drill penetration in less than an hour. Alert me to any status changes. Skinner out."

The radio chirped again, and Skinner returned it to his pocket. He holstered his gun, and then he pulled a few instruments out of his suit, sensors and other devices. Eleanor recognized one of them as a telluric scanner.

"Now," he said, "before we return to the surface, I'd like to get a better look at this thing."

"Aaron," her mother said, "don't do this. The Concentrator—"

"Do *not* attempt to escape," he said, ignoring her. "Or you will force me to shoot you."

With that, he marched back down into the crater,

toward the Concentrator. He approached it, checking his instruments, and then circled around it. Eleanor felt a shift in the telluric currents as he did so, as though the Concentrator were responding to his probing.

It seemed to be waking up.

— CHAPTER —
23

"IT'S OVER," ELEANOR'S MOTHER WHISPERED.

Eleanor strained a little against the zip tie but couldn't budge it. "There has to be something we can do."

"There isn't. It's too late. I'm so sorry, sweetie. I should never have sent you those files. If I'd thought for one minute that you would—"

"It's not your fault," Eleanor said, while below them, Skinner seemed to have become lost in his study of the Concentrator. "We know whose fault it is."

The hum continued to build in response to Skinner's instruments. But after a few moments, Eleanor felt something else moving beneath its current, like a squirming larva within its cocoon. Something inside the black tree. Every time Eleanor had interacted with the Concentrator, she had become more aware of . . . it. But it was hard to really grasp what it was with the hum so deafening. It felt as though it had reached her bones, and she moaned a little.

"Sweetie, what's wrong?" her mother asked.

"It's the Concentrator," Eleanor said. "I . . . feel it."

"What do you mean you feel it?"

"I always have. Since I came here." Just then, Eleanor felt a tremble in the ground. A drum-like pounding, growing closer. It wasn't the humming of the telluric currents. This was something else. "And I don't think I'm the only one." Kixi was coming their way. Eleanor thought back to the mammoth's agitation. "Skinner needs to stop. Now."

Her mother was silent a moment but then called out, "Aaron! Please, stop this! You don't know what you're dealing with!"

"Do *you*?" he called back. "Or do you believe in your daughter's notion of aliens driving rogue planets around?" When her mother made no reply to that, he lifted the scanner. "I truly wish I could've counted on you to help me, Dr. Perry. But I am prepared to do this alone. Now if you'll excuse me, I must dial up the gain and check for subcurrents."

As soon as he adjusted the scanner, the hum became overwhelming, just as it had when Eleanor's mother had done the same thing. Kixi bellowed from somewhere very nearby, the thunder of her approach growing louder.

Skinner looked up from the scanner. "What in God's name was that?"

In the next moment, Kixi erupted from a nearby wash, charging toward Eleanor and her mother like an avalanche of muscle and fur, tusks held high, trumpeting in anger. She charged up the hill to the crater's rim, right past the Perrys.

At the sight of her, Skinner's eyes and mouth opened wide. Kixi roared downward, right for him. He fumbled for the gun at his side but failed to pull it from his holster before Kixi reached him. A sideways swipe of her tusk sent him flying through the air. He landed in a heap, but he was still alive and struggling to get up. Kixi was on him before he could, trampling him under her massive feet again and again, rolling him and folding him, breaking him until he stopped moving.

The humming quieted. Only then did the mammoth stop, shaking her head and huffing, whatever spell she'd been under now broken. She sniffed and probed Skinner's body with her trunk, as if confused or surprised by it. Then Kixi turned toward Eleanor and her mother and lumbered toward them with her usual gait.

"Eleanor," her mother whispered, her voice terrified.

"Don't worry, Mom," Eleanor said. "She's herself again. We're safe." When the mammoth reached them, she gently laid her trunk on Eleanor's shoulder. "See? Now, how're we going to get free?"

"There's a knife in the left pocket of my suit, if you can reach it."

Eleanor extended her hands behind her as far as they could go and rooted her way into the first pocket she found.

"Not that one," her mother said. "The next one down."

Eleanor found the right one and felt the blade, a small pocketknife. She pulled it out, managed to open it, and carefully cut the zip tie from her mother's wrists. Then her mother turned around and did the same for her.

Eleanor rose to her feet and gave Kixi's trunk a hug. "Thank you," she whispered. "Thank you, girl."

Kixi touched Eleanor's cheek with the velvet tip of her trunk.

"Oh, Aaron," her mother whispered, looking over at the scientist's body. "If only you had listened."

"You tried, Mom," Eleanor said.

Her mother nodded and took a deep breath. "We need to get back to the Concentrator."

"Why?"

"When you and Skinner arrived, I had just found what I think is a control panel of some kind. I was trying to see if I could use it to shut the Concentrator down."

"Okay, but . . ." Eleanor glanced over at Skinner's ruined body. "It's over, isn't it?"

"No. The G.E.T. will be back, and next time, we won't be able to stop them. Skinner drove the G.E.T.'s experimental energy program, but you heard what he said—this 'Preservation Protocol,' as he called it, is UN policy now. The G.E.T. board of directors will find someone else to continue his work."

"Who's the head of the board of directors?"

"The chairman. His name is Charles Watkins."

Watkins? Where had Eleanor heard that name before?

"Come on," her mother said.

They left Kixi at the top of the crater and descended to the Concentrator. Her mother led her around to the far side of the trunk, where Eleanor saw a circular panel of porous metal with a series of bumps and divots.

"I think these are buttons or switches of some

kind," her mother said. "But I have no idea what they do or how they work."

Eleanor didn't either, but as she approached the object, she felt the sensation from her dream return, of being cradled in its branches. She inhaled deeply to clear away the residue of fear over Skinner and tuned in to the hum, tracing the currents flowing around her into the Concentrator. She laid her hand on the panel, feeling its contours, trying to make some sense of them.

She felt the larva move in her mind, reaching back. Almost a shock, but not painful. A *force*, responding to her through her hand, climbing up her muscles.

She recoiled, yanking her hand away.

"What is it?" her mother asked.

"I— It's . . . alive."

"What?"

"No." Eleanor chewed on her lip. "Not quite alive. Aware, maybe."

Her mother took a step away from the structure, casting it a wary eye. "What do you mean *aware*?"

Eleanor rubbed the hand that had touched the console. "It's what I was telling you. I can feel it. I think Kixi felt it, too. That's why she attacked Skinner. The Concentrator reaches out."

Her mother shook her head. "I don't like this.

Perhaps this was a mistake."

Eleanor didn't like it either. She hated this black thing spreading its limbs over her. Hated it the way she hated snakes and spiders, but magnified exponentially. It was as if the Concentrator struck the instinctual fear buried deep in her genetic memory. But fear was actually too simple a word. Fear of the unknown could be tempered by knowing it. But what Eleanor felt now was a horror at the *unknowable*.

Was this how Amarok had felt, staring at the spheres of Polaris Station in their slow march across the ice? Either way, he had decided to fight. How could Eleanor do any less? And if the Concentrator could reach out, to Kixi and her, did that mean Eleanor could reach *in*?

She laid her hand on the panel again, ignoring her mother's protests, prepared this time as the same force insinuated itself through her arm. She closed her eyes, trying to keep the presence contained, as it covered her mind like an oil slick.

Once she allowed the connection with the Concentrator, she began to glimpse a little of how it fit together, but at the deep, almost unconscious level of intuition. With her thoughts, Eleanor tugged at its roots, reaching deep into the earth like a tumor. She observed its intent, the fearful calculations of its aim.

She caressed its controls, empowered but disgusted by them, bending its function to her will.

First, she changed the alignment of its roots so that it ceased the gathering of telluric currents. Then, to shut it down, she killed the squirming, fragmentary awareness embedded in the Concentrator's machinery. It was easy, like pulling a grub out of the grass and crushing it between her fingers.

Her connection with the alien device collapsed, and the oil slick over her mind cleared away, the Concentrator a lifeless monument to the inscrutable force that had created it.

Eleanor opened her eyes.

"It's done," she said.

Her mom blinked. "How . . . ?" She looked at the console. "You were working the controls. It responded to you."

"I shut it down," Eleanor said.

"But how?"

"I don't know." She didn't know why she was able to sense the hum, why she saw the dark planet, or why the Concentrator had obeyed her. But she was, she did, and it had.

A loud cracking sounded overhead, close enough to thunder that Eleanor thought of lightning. She glanced up. A seam had appeared in the cavern's ceiling, and as she looked, it spread, like a chip in a windshield.

"Mom?" she said.

"We have to get out of here. Now."

They ran from the crater, up the hill to where Kixi stood grazing.

"What's going on?" Eleanor asked.

"I don't know," her mother said. "The energy from the Concentrator must have been sustaining the cavern. Now it's gone."

A second crack appeared, larger than the first. Chunks of ice rained down from it onto the tundra. Kixi's eyes rolled, looking everywhere, her small, flappy ears twitching.

"There's nothing we can do," her mother said. "We have to run."

Eleanor nodded and tugged on Kixi's fur. "Come on, girl. You have to come with us."

The mammoth took a few uncertain steps and then broke into a trot, following Eleanor and her mother as they ran across the tundra toward the canyon. Before they'd even reached the village, three new cracks had appeared, joining up with the first, dropping boulders and icebergs that shook the ground when they struck.

Kixi trumpeted, batting at Eleanor with her trunk.

"I know, girl," she said.

They were still a distance from the canyon, and even if they made it, they would have to climb the crevasse, and Eleanor worried about its stability with the ceiling caving in.

A chunk of ice the size of a car landed on one of the mammoth-bone huts right next to them, crushing it and splintering its massive bones. Kixi bellowed but kept to Eleanor's side, even though the mammoth could have run faster. Kixi had charged Skinner with overwhelming speed, but she was staying with Eleanor and her mom, as if waiting for them.

Up ahead, the canyon opened. Next to it was Amarok's other sled. The sight of it gave Eleanor an idea, and she ran for it.

"Kixi!" she said. "Kixi, come here! You're going to help us, okay?"

The mammoth followed her, and Eleanor gathered the coils of leather cord that normally harnessed a team of ten wolves, then asked her mom to help. Together, they tied the ropes around the mammoth's waist. Kixi stamped her feet a little but let them do it, and a few moments later, Eleanor and her mother climbed onto the sled.

On the far side of the cavern, a whole section of the

wall sloughed off, like the shelf of an iceberg falling into the sea.

Eleanor grabbed onto the sled. "Okay, Kixi, run!" she shouted, but the mammoth stood rooted in place. "Kixi!"

"Here," her mom said. She picked up Amarok's whip and gave it a swing over her head, but it took a couple of tries before it cracked near Kixi's rear end.

The mammoth's legs quivered with a startled little jump, and she lurched forward at a trot, dragging the sled behind her.

"Faster, Kixi!" Eleanor said.

Her mom cracked the whip again, and the mammoth broke into a gallop, straight into the canyon, the crevasse barely wide enough for her enormous frame.

Up they rose, climbing as fast as Amarok's wolves. Behind them, they heard the cracking and thunder continue as the cavern came down. It seemed the whole thing would collapse any moment.

"Good girl, Kixi!" Eleanor called in a voice she used for puppies. "Faster! Faster!"

The mammoth trumpeted, galloping upward, sometimes breaking right through the sides of the canyon with her broad shoulders when it became too narrow. The minutes and the distance passed slowly but steadily.

At last, Eleanor sighted a slice of sky overhead. "We're almost there!"

She and her mother put on their masks, and soon they burst onto the surface. Kixi stopped abruptly, the sled careening to the side, almost spilling Eleanor and her mom. In the distance, they saw the silver spheres of Polaris Station, while Amarok's people, his wolves, and the station crew raced toward them in an indistinct mob.

Just then, the ground shook with a tremor, and a few minutes later, the first of the runners reached them. Eleanor had to smile at the look of shock on the faces of the station crew when they passed Kixi and kept going, fleeing the weakening ground. Soon, Eleanor spotted Finn, Julian, and their dad. Between them, they supported a wounded Amarok, who could barely keep up.

"Finn!" Eleanor shouted. "Bring him here!"

"What's going on down there?" Dr. Powers asked, out of breath, as they reached the sled.

"The cavern is collapsing," Eleanor's mother said. "Eleanor shut down the Concentrator."

Dr. Powers nodded, appearing somewhat confused as he helped lay Amarok down on the sled. Then they all climbed on, Eleanor's mother gave the whip another crack, and Kixi pulled them forward.

"Skinner?" Finn asked.

"Dead," Eleanor said. "He was messing with the Concentrator."

"But a mammoth got in his way," her mother said.

Kixi hauled them a short distance, and a minute later, the cracking sound behind them grew frantic and deafening. Eleanor looked back to see plumes of ice and snow shooting hundreds of feet in the air, the spheres of the station beginning to sink, tipping inward against one another with the squealing of tortured metal. Then the ground opened up with a *boom* that seemed to ripple the ice beneath the sled, and the station vanished with the rest of the ice sheet into a gaping hole a mile wide.

No one said anything. They just stared. Tears had started down the side of Amarok's cheek but had frozen there along the way, and Eleanor grieved with him. In an instant, he had just witnessed his entire world buried under a mountain of ice.

After the ground had settled, Amarok's people regrouped near the edge of the crater, tending to their wounded and their dying, reverent at the grave of their village and those who had been caught in the collapse. The hired hands of the station crew had collected some distance away and seemed to have lost all interest in their former captives.

Eleanor and her mom told Finn, Julian, and Dr. Powers what had happened in the cavern with Skinner, but when it came time to explain how Eleanor had shut down the Concentrator, she couldn't find the right words. To describe it would've required a language she didn't know.

"The Preservation Protocol?" Dr. Powers asked.

Eleanor's mom leaned over Amarok, pushing aside his devoted wolves so she could tend to the warrior's wound. "That's what he called it."

"They can't hide it forever," Dr. Powers said. "It's a *planet*."

"They've kept it secret so far," Eleanor said. "And look at the damage they've caused already."

"True," Dr. Powers said, then turned to Eleanor's mother and gestured to Amarok. "How is he?"

"The bullet passed clean through," she said. "It didn't break any bones on its way. I think he will heal, especially if the effects of the energy linger with him. Though I can't say the same for some of the others. I should help tend to them."

She got up to leave, but Amarok took her hand, which was covered in his dried blood, and squeezed it. "Thank you."

"You're welcome," she said. "But I am so sorry about your home."

He closed his eyes a moment, nodded, and then said, "You go. Night soon."

He was right. They were in the middle of nowhere, miles and miles from Barrow, without shelter or supplies, none of their suits had power, and they didn't possess Amarok's resistance to the cold.

"Sam," Dr. Powers said, "do you still have the Sync? Could we contact Barrow?"

"Possibly." Eleanor's mother dug into a pocket in her suit and pulled out Eleanor's device, but her body sagged when she looked at it. "Oh, no."

"What is it?" Eleanor asked.

"The cell signal is dead."

"I thought the Sync could communicate anywhere in the world," Julian said. "Isn't that the point?"

"Only with the quantum twin," her mother said. "For normal connections, it used regular cell towers and satellites. Polaris Station had its own relay, but now that's gone. I have no way to reach Barrow."

"It's okay," Dr. Powers said. "It'll be okay. Someone from Barrow should be here soon. They had to feel that—it was practically an earthquake. They're going to want to know what happened."

He was probably right, and that reassured Eleanor. But what did that mean for Amarok and his people? Where could they go? What would they do?

She looked down at Amarok and found him smiling at her from the sled. "Make new home," he said, as if he'd read her mind. Then, in his own language, he called his people to him, and they gathered around the sled. He spoke to them for several moments. Many of them wept openly, but under the influence of their leader's voice, their shoulders rose and their backs straightened. When Amarok finished, they moved with determination and purpose. A few of them untied the sled from Kixi, then harnessed up Amarok's wolves. There were only six of them.

Before long, they'd assembled together, some of the wounded on the sled with Amarok, others limping along with help. Amarok smiled at Eleanor's mother and the others. "Good-bye," he said, and with one last glance at Eleanor, "Make new home."

Then he and his people marched forward as one, away from the crater, toward the horizon. Eleanor watched them diminish in the distance until their individual silhouettes merged into a single moving shadow, Kixi a shuffling bulge in the middle.

"What's going to happen to them?" Finn asked.

"Whatever it is," Julian said, "it'll be on their terms.

You gotta respect that."

He had a point, but Eleanor felt something else. Watching that wounded, beleaguered village marching across the ice, diminishing with each step, she thought of what Skinner had said, the future he had described. Tribes like Amarok's, gone. Cities like Phoenix, gone. Whole cultures and civilizations, erased. Humanity reduced to a small group of survivors, chosen by the G.E.T., eking out an existence on a barren, frozen planet for as long as they could, with no real hope.

Well, those were not Eleanor's terms. That was not the future she wanted.

In the next moment, Amarok's people were gone, swallowed up in the empty vastness of the glacier, lost to the ice once more.

— CHAPTER —
24

THE COLD DESCENDED ON THEM RAPIDLY. BUT AFTER everything they'd been through, Eleanor wasn't about to let it win at the end. She gnashed and growled inside, fighting back the cold with her mind, even as her body weakened and went numb.

They had all gathered together, forming a tight circle, shoulder to shoulder, to conserve body heat, teeth chattering, clapping hands, stamping feet. Off in the distance, the crew of Polaris Station did the same. But soon they mustered and moved, setting out over the ice in the direction of Barrow, and a short while later they disappeared.

At one point, Eleanor's mother leaned in to Dr. Powers. "I've been monitoring my symptoms. Hypothermia will set in soon," she whispered.

He put his arm around her. "Someone will come. Hang in there, Sam."

But as the afternoon sun fell closer and closer to the horizon, and Eleanor lost feeling in her feet, she began to wonder if the cold had finally been given the time it needed to take her and all of them. Its waiting game had paid off.

"Perhaps we should start walking, too," her mother said. "Toward Barrow."

"No," Dr. Powers said. "Here, near the crater, is our best chance of being spotted."

That made sense, but Eleanor felt the cold robbing her hope. She remembered all the times it had assaulted her—in the tunnel, and after she'd run from Skinner. She realized it had only been running her down, exhausting her with its lethal strategy.

Just then, the distant sound of an engine whined along the ice toward them. They all looked at one another, then leaped to their feet, scanning the horizon and the sky.

"Do you see anything?" Julian asked.

"Nothing," Dr. Powers said.

But the sound was real, growing louder, getting closer, and a few moments later, Finn pointed up in the sky and exclaimed, "There!"

It was a small plane, with runners along its belly, able to land and take off on the ice. As it neared the crater, it dipped low, and Eleanor and the others began to jump, flail their arms, and shout at it.

"Hey!"

"Down here!"

"Help us!"

The plane circled a couple of times around the crater in a lazy arc, showing no sign that its pilot had noticed the people stranded down below, and Eleanor began to worry that any moment, it would head back to Barrow, leaving them to die. But in one last pass, the pilot took the circle a little wider, flying almost directly over Eleanor and the others. They jumped and screamed at its belly, then its tail.

"Did they see us?" Finn asked. "Did they?"

"They had to," Dr. Powers said, and he was right.

The plane swung out far and banked, lining up for an approach, then came in for a landing very close to where Eleanor and the rest stood waiting. As soon as it reached a stop, they all rushed toward it.

As Eleanor approached the craft, the door opened, and a familiar face appeared, covered in stubble.

"Did you guys make that mess?" Luke asked, pointing at the crater.

Eleanor couldn't believe it. How was he here? How did he know? "We did," she said as she boarded the plane with the others. "Are you impressed?"

"Very," he said, and pulled her into a quick, back-slapping hug. "Good to see you, kid."

"Good to see you, too," Eleanor said.

When they were all onboard and seated, Luke closed the main door and returned to his open cockpit. "I take it these two are Dr. Perry and Dr. Powers?"

"We are," Eleanor's mother said. "And you are?"

"This is Luke Fournier, Mom," Eleanor said. "If it wasn't for him, I would never have found you."

"Then I am very grateful to you, Mr. Fournier," her mother said.

"Just Luke," he said, facing forward for takeoff. "And if it wasn't for your daughter, I'd probably be kicking back with a warm drink in Phoenix right now. So let's get going."

A few moments later, airborne, Eleanor was able to see the full scale of the crater. It looked as if a meteor had struck the ice sheet. The open pit, wider than a football stadium, dropped hundreds and hundreds of feet from the surface to a jagged field of icy rubble at the bottom. In shutting down the Concentrator,

Eleanor had left a terrible, gaping wound on the ice sheet from which it would not easily heal.

She found a measure of satisfaction in that.

On the short flight back to Barrow, Luke explained how he had ended up at the crater, circling. It turned out the whole town had felt the impact of the cavern collapse, just as Dr. Powers had expected they would, and several pilots had wanted to investigate. But the G.E.T. had seized the airport and grounded everyone.

"Whatever had happened out there," he said, "they didn't want anyone to see it." He turned around and looked back into the cabin with a crooked grin. "Which naturally meant that I *had* to. So I, uh, borrowed this little girl and got in the air as quick as I could. Bit dicey at takeoff, though. Bastards actually tried to shoot me down."

"We are very grateful you risked it," Eleanor's mother said.

"I admit," Luke said, "I wasn't expecting to find you all alive."

Eleanor rolled her eyes. "Thanks a lot."

"The G.E.T. won't show any of us mercy, going forward," Dr. Powers said, and a somber silence took hold of the aircraft.

He was right. They were outlaws now. The G.E.T.

might even try to hunt them down for what they knew, to ensure their silence and maintain the UN's so-called Preservation Protocol. They would have to go into hiding somewhere.

Eleanor grabbed her mother's arm with a sudden panic. "We need to warn Uncle Jack!"

"As soon as we get to Barrow," she said, nodding.

"So what happened down there?" Luke asked.

Eleanor and the others just looked at one another, not sure where to start. But Eleanor took the lead, explaining everything, aware of how impossible it all sounded. But Luke just kept nodding along, occasionally glancing back at her. His eyebrows stayed pressed together, except the few times his eyes widened, but he seemed to be taking it all in. Maybe it was the fact that there were four other people, two of them scientists, nodding along in agreement.

When she finished, Luke rubbed the whiskers on his chin for a solid minute, thinking. Then he said, "So there's aliens up there on some planet? Right now?"

Eleanor thought back to her vision of the dark world. Its terrible surface had felt . . . dead. Long, long dead. "I don't *think* so," she said. "I think the planet and the Concentrators are running on their own. Automatically."

"So where are the others?" Luke asked.

321

"The others?" Eleanor's mother said.

"The other Concentrators," Luke said. "There's gotta be more than one, right? Probably several. I don't imagine this rogue planet would come all this way to suck power from one little hose. You said there were lots of these, uh, telluric whatevers, running around the earth?"

"Yes," Eleanor whispered. What Luke said made sense. "Mom, do you still have the Sync?" Her mom nodded and handed it to her. The device's cell connection might be dead, but Eleanor could still access its data, and she opened the file with the map of the world. "Look," she said, pointing. "There are all these lines intersecting here in Alaska. But look over here." She traced a line to Egypt. "There are just as many here."

"And there," Finn said, jabbing Peru.

There were several such intersections around the globe, all of them possessing a strong convergence of telluric current. But there was something else they all had in common. They were places von Albrecht had written about.

Gradually, Eleanor began to form a theory of her own. "What if aliens visited the earth tens of thousands of years ago to prepare it for their planet? All these places have something in common. Some people think they were built by aliens. Like the Great Pyramids. Well, maybe the aliens planted Concentrators at all these sites, and then they left, and now the dark world has come to harvest the energy!"

Everyone fell into silence again, listening to the purr of the plane's engines.

"We'll reach Barrow soon," Luke said. "I'm going to land far outside of town, or the G.E.T. might try to shoot us down again."

"Do you know anywhere we can hide?" Dr. Powers asked.

"Felipe?" Eleanor suggested.

Luke nodded. "You kidding? Aliens? He'll love this."

"Then what?" Julian asked.

"Then we jailbreak my plane," Luke said. "Head to Fairbanks. Betty can hide us for a little while. From there . . ."

From there, Eleanor thought, *we have to travel around the world to those other sites*. It sounded like an overwhelming mission, an impossible task, but then, that was exactly what people would have said about Eleanor's trip to the Arctic to search for her mom. Yet she had found her, and her mom was here, sitting in the seat next to her, alive and safe.

If there were other Concentrators, they would find

them, and Eleanor knew now how to shut them down. If they succeeded in that, if the rogue world could no longer drain the earth's energy, would it die? Or at least leave their solar system and move on?

A new vision of the future filled Eleanor's mind, an alternative to Skinner's dire apocalypse. A vision of an earth returned to its orbit, a world of warmth and thaw and hope.

"From there, what?" Finn asked, in response to Luke's open question.

"From there," Eleanor said, thinking of Amarok's smile, "we make a new home."

⟶ ACKNOWLEDGMENTS ⟶

THE WRITING OF A BOOK IS, FOR ME, VERY MUCH A TEAM effort in which there are no unimportant contributions. To thank everyone involved never ceases to cause me anxiety for fear of forgetting someone. Nevertheless, here goes.

Thank you to Donna Bray for giving me the opportunity to go with Eleanor on this amazing journey. This book is only the beginning. Thanks also to Jordan Brown, who asked all the right questions and helped me find the right answers. From the beginning, he and I were on the same storytelling page. Also invaluable to me has been the amazing community of writers and friends here in Utah. I can't possibly name them all, so instead I'll give a general shout-out to Rock Canyon. I could not have written this book without the support of my wife, Jaime, who not only understands and accepts the inevitability of my procrastination but stands ready to read and talk about what I'm writing. Appreciation must also be expressed for my stepkids, Stuart, Sophie, and Charlie, whose excitement for my books gets me excited, too. Thank you to Steve, my agent and partner in this career I still sometimes can't believe I have. Lastly, thank you to all alien beings who may have visited this planet at points in the past. I hope you'll forgive me if I've mischaracterized your intent in this book, or failed to give you proper credit for the monolithic structures you helped to build.